THE
QUARTZ TOWER

KINGDOMS OF OZ BOOK 2

CARRIE WHITETHORNE

Editing by Elemental Editing Services
Cover design by Deranged Doctor Designs
Proof Reading by Zoe's Author Services
Formatting by Kassie Morse

"Consider yourself..."
Wrong musical.

For my long-suffering husband.
Your patience is astounding.
Thank you.

CHAPTER 1

$\mathcal{I}$ was in the courtyard, watching. Remi still wasn't back. The sun had risen, and the cloudless sky was blue. The longer I watched and waited, the more anxious I felt.

Fallon was leaning on the wall beside the door to the north tower. Wearing his usual leather pants and vest, he was perfectly relaxed and just observing me. Tilting his head, he held out his hand.

"Where?" I queried, assuming he wanted me to go with him.

He opened the door and waited for me to walk through.

"Up?"

He nodded, left the door open, and followed me as I climbed the spiral staircase. It was identical to the tower housing my room, and the one Fallon slept in, except the staircase led directly into a circular room holding a large throne-like chair and a large, crystal orb. That was all—at first glance, anyway.

Recalling the crystal ball my great grandmother had described in her book, I raised my brows in recognition.

"Is this...?"

He nodded.

"I can see anything, anywhere in Oz?" I asked, running my fingertips over the smooth globe.

It clouded instantly, filling with a white fog. I peered into the smoke but couldn't make anything out.

"Same theory as the shoes?" I inquired, as he stepped to my side.

He placed his hand on the small of my back, and I thought of Remi.

The smoke swirled then cleared and his face appeared.

"But where is he?"

I wasn't asking anyone in particular, but the image changed, showing me a different picture. Remi was on the back of a Lioneag. He didn't look afraid and I recognized the creature carrying him.

"Is anyone with him?" I asked urgently. I'd sent him for a reason, but I wanted proof he hadn't just been sent home alone.

The image changed again, showing me another mount. The black, feathered bird carried a single rider. She wasn't wearing armor this time, but a pair of flowing pants and a matching shirt instead. Her blonde hair flew behind her as the bird raced toward the border.

I looked at Fallon with my eyes wide. "She's coming with him. Now."

He didn't look concerned, instead he moved over to the window as if to watch.

"Will she get past the thing I put up yesterday?" I asked, joining him.

He shrugged and put his arm around my shoulders, squeezing gently.

"I'm not afraid of her, Fallon, I just don't want a repeat of... well, you know."

I turned away, looking back to the now clear ball. That was useful. That was incredibly useful. I remembered Sayer had mentioned it, but he didn't give it as much credence as the slippers. I made a mental note to go back and practice using it later. "Come on, I should get ready for her. If she doesn't land and tear everything apart, she'll probably expect tea or something."

* * *

DANIEL CHOSE another of the soldiers to go with him to escort my guest to the fortress. I felt bad not knowing his name, but thanked him for helping as I set the table for a late lunch. I wasn't really hungry, but I was sure Fallon and Tatiana would be. He'd taken himself off to the kitchen, I didn't know what for because there wasn't much in the way of food in there and I didn't have a store to run to for supplies.

It was the first time I'd used my table. I'd created it with grandeur in mind, something I'd never had before. The smaller table I'd eaten at with Glinda, Sayer, and Fallon was more intimate—too intimate, given how Glinda behaved toward Fallon.

This shouted formality. Boundaries. Power.

I ran my hand over the wood, admiring the craftsmanship and wondering who had actually made it when I heard the door open.

Remi's voice carried into the room, and I went to greet him and my guest.

"Lady Ellana, may I present the Lady Tatiana, Witch of the North," he announced with a bow.

I smiled at him and patted his shoulder. "Thanks. That isn't your job. I appreciate you going all that way for me."

He nodded and stepped back. "Is there anything else you require, my lady?"

"Will you stay for lunch?" I asked, knowing his answer before he gave it. When he shook his head, I spoke before he could. "Okay. You must be exhausted, go home and get some rest. I'll be fine here."

Tatiana had remained silent during our exchange. I was aware of her standing there, watching me. I could feel her eyes on me, but I ignored her until I was done. How I handled my people was my business, and I was done keeping up pretenses. She'd demonstrated her willingness to meet with me again by coming here, so she clearly wanted to know who I was. And at this rate, I was more than happy to be myself instead of playing mind games.

When I did look at her, I smiled. "Hi. Thanks for coming, I know it's short notice, but you said if I needed anything and, well, I do."

Her straight, blonde hair sat just above her shoulders. Her blue eyes shone as she smiled at me, and all the tension and hostility of our previous meeting was gone. "Not at all. I'm glad you invited me. I wanted the opportunity to clear the air."

Her previous appearance in my lands had sent my guards into a frenzy. They'd defended their home with no encouragement from me and I'd been forced to halt the battle when her Lioneag had slaughtered dozens of my men. I was still pissed about it. "Yeah. Well, the dead are being tended to by their families and funerals are being arranged," I commented flatly.

She had the decency to look apologetic. "Yes, Remi told me," she replied, abashed.

4

I wanted to ask if that was it? If that was all she had to say after all the chaos and death she had caused. Except, I'd invited her to build a bridge and find out what no one seemed able to tell me, not to start a fight, however much I wanted to. "If you want to come with me, we'll have lunch ready soon. You must be hungry after your journey," I offered, giving her what I hoped was a welcoming smile.

She smiled in return and I turned away to head toward the kitchen, wondering what Fallon had managed to scrape together for lunch.

"What role have you assigned him?" she queried, pulling my attention back to her.

I didn't quite understand her question and it must have been clear from my expression when I looked back at her, with my brow raised.

"Fallon," she clarified.

"He's... I haven't assigned him any role. That isn't how I work," I told her, not wanting to be caught at a loss for words.

She tilted her head and a small line formed between her brows. "No? What about the general?"

I gave her a sharp look, not liking her belligerent tone at all, and she grimaced. "I didn't mean for that to sound..." She let out a frustrated breath and looked down at her clothes. "I'm not here to fight. Believe it or not, Ellana, I am here to help."

She sounded sincere. At least, there was none of the seemingly forced and brittle sweetness her sister shoved down my throat every time we met, and the barrier had let her through. She obviously didn't have hostile intentions. But then again, neither did Glinda, apparently. I didn't trust her any more than I trusted the cream puff, but I was interested to see how this witch thought she could help me. Hell, she'd just killed a load of my people. The war that had torn Oz apart was just as much her mess as it was Glinda's. She owed me something.

"Remi presented himself already in the role. Fallon hasn't given any indication of what he wants to do, yet. For all I know, he wants to leave here and I wouldn't blame him. It isn't as though he can tell me."

It was an honest answer. I didn't expect her to respond with, "Have you asked him?"

"No," I admitted, glancing around to see if he was there. "I try not to ask questions that require more than a yes or no answer."

That last wasn't entirely true. He could communicate well enough for me to understand him, and she was aware of that. "Ask him. You may be surprised by the answer." There was a mild challenge in her tone.

She was watching me and I wasn't sure which conclusions she was drawing about me, but whatever they were, it seemed they weren't negative. I was still going to be cautious with her though.

I started walking toward the kitchen, and called out over my shoulder, "You can wait here or follow, but I'm going to fix lunch."

"I'll help," she offered.

The temptation to turn and look at her was immense, but I managed to keep walking, pushing open the door to the kitchen and stepping inside.

"Oh, you're here," I commented when I noticed Fallon.

He was in the process of setting out plates of what appeared to be very small pastries, and he looked up at me with a broad smile.

"Where did they come from?"

He pushed a large terrine of soup toward me and I lifted

the lid. "Orla," I answered, recognizing the contents of the bowl. "How long has she been sending things up here?"

He shrugged, looking past me to Tatiana.

"Fallon," she said in greeting.

His lips twitched up in a half smile and I mouthed, "What?" His head tipped to the side, indicating he was pleased to see her, and Tatiana cleared her throat.

"While I took responsibility for these lands after my sister's... passing, it was Fallon who was left to maintain some sort of order here," she explained behind me. "I was conscious of the danger of involving myself in these lands. These are not *my* people. I want the best for them, but they are not mine to govern. In the absence of a witch, the role fell to Fallon's family. In the absence of a steward and with Fallon reluctant to officially fill the role, it was something of a difficult task."

I hadn't looked away from Fallon while she spoke, watching his expression change from relaxed and friendly to tense when she mentioned his family. But I turned then, and challenged, "So it was you who locked him up here?"

Her eyes flicked to me then back to him. "He chose to stay."

"You left him here alone," I argued in his defense.

His hand settled on my shoulder and Tatiana continued, "When he's ready, he'll tell you the truth of what happened. I left him alone here because I had no choice. If I interfered, if your army formed an allegiance with me, things would have gone even more badly than they already had. This was the only way to maintain a tentative peace in Oz."

I looked to Fallon for his reaction. He nodded once and pointed to the food, apparently willing to move on from the conversation. I wasn't happy, but I supposed I should get lunch underway. "Take a plate. We'll just lay it all out and help ourselves," I suggested.

If she was bothered by my lack of formality, she didn't show it. She simply grabbed two plates and followed me back to the dining room.

When the table was full, I looked at the pair of them and directed, "Take a seat, help yourselves."

Fallon waited for me to sit down before serving me a bowl of soup. I opened my mouth to protest, but Tatiana interjected, "No point in arguing with him, he'll just do it more," and picked up a small pastry. "I should ask Orla to show Bree how to make these," she commented, seemingly more to herself.

"Bree?" I prompted, picking up a bread roll and tearing it in half.

Tatiana nodded. "My... well, I suppose she's my steward."

I nodded and dipped my roll into my soup. "So," I began after a few mouthfuls, "as nice as this is, behaving like two old friends having lunch, I should probably get to why I invited you here."

Tati nodded once.

"What do you want from me?" I asked flatly.

Tatiana looked at Fallon, smiled, and said, "I like her. Do you like her? Never mind, that was a stupid question, you haven't shot her." Then she looked to me and continued, "I need you to take the Quartz Tower."

I hadn't had the time to test the power I'd been granted from taking the fortress, and while I assumed the process would be the same in the East, I'd had enough trouble getting into the fortress. What would the Quartz Tower be like? Also, why would she be so keen for me to take on even more power, and what was in it for her? I glanced to Fallon and noticed he was looking at me expectantly. "Why?"

Tatiana stood up and leaned over the table to ladle soup into her own bowl, replying, "As it stands, the three of us—you, Glinda, and myself—are on an equal footing. We each have a stronghold, we each have a considerable amount of power bestowed upon us, and we each have our own agenda. I also know you are your own person, Ellana. You offer me no allegiance, and I can tell you do not suffer fools gladly, which rules my sister out as a trusted ally. So, in the interests of the people of Oz, I want you to take your place as guardian of the east and set yourself above the both of us."

I frowned. There had to be some sort of catch. I couldn't see either sister easily giving me more control and power than either of them wielded. "Why?" I repeated, sounding like a broken record.

She sat down, stirring her soup, apparently unconcerned by what she had just stated. "Because without a stable leader here in Oz, there is no one to keep those with power in check."

"Yourself included?"

She smiled, nodded once, and ate a spoonful of soup.

Fallon didn't react, continuing with his lunch as though we were discussing the decor, and he seemed to be making a point of not looking my way.

What the hell was that? Why would Tatiana want me to overpower her? Why did Fallon look as though he expected it?

Putting my spoon down, I leaned my elbows on the table and speculated, "I like a good manipulation tactic as much as the next girl, but this is a bit above the stakes I'm used to playing with. You want me to take all the power and you want me to protect your world, but what's in it for you?"

Leaning back in her chair, she looked me directly in the eyes, and stated, "My people, my family, are in the north. When my sisters were killed, by your grand-mother I might add, I was forced to take guardianship of some of their people, and I have been more than happy to do so, but what followed..." Her eyes darkened, and she took a steadying breath before continuing, "The Emerald City was lost, sacked and burned. The Wizard, a peaceful man who helped so many, burned with it. Millions of people have died. I did my best, but it was never enough, and while I know I should have done more, taken more risks, done more damage, I was unable to. As much as I hate what she has become, Glinda is my sister, and I cannot bring myself to serve the justice she deserves. But you, Ellana, if your power outstrips hers, can tip the balance. You can return Oz to its former glory." She glanced to Fallon. "You have the support and you have the right values to rule if you take what is yours. I have full trust in you. I know you can undo much of the damage and give our people, all the people of Oz, the hope and strength to rebuild. All you have to do is stop her."

She went back to her soup after that little speech, leaving me to mull over her words and find a response.

I didn't really know what to say. How do you respond to that? She'd just laid the blame entirely at Glinda's feet. For everything. Did that mean Glinda really had orchestrated poor Dorothy's involvement here? Had my suspicions been correct? If Tatiana was to be believed, and Fallon didn't look as though he disagreed with any of her claims, then why had Glinda brought me here? Surely she knew all of this too? What did Glinda have planned? Despite all the questions whirling in my head, all I managed to blurt was, "You want me to kill your sister?"

Tatiana shrugged. "I'd rather you didn't, but if I'm going

to be sensible, the important thing is that she's stopped. If that ends in her demise, then so be it."

I looked at her in disbelief.

"I have a duty here, Ellana. I took an oath—"

"You people and your damned oaths," I snapped, thinking of Sayer and the oath keeping him with the Sugarplum Fairy who, according to her sister, was the cause of all this destruction. "That shit died out with knights and castles where I'm from, except for doctors and lawyers, but their jobs are kind of important. I mean, seriously, swearing an oath to serve Your Magicness dinner every evening promptly at seven? Who does that?"

Fallon was smirking by the time I was done with my outburst, while Tatiana pressed her lips together in a thin line and looked sideways at him, trying not to laugh.

"What?" I demanded, looking between them. "Everything about this place is ridiculous and it's looking like I've been dragged here to make some sort of sense of it before all of you kill the poor people at your mercy. The insult is, I wasn't even consulted. Sayer just followed Glinda's orders, brought me here and left me to it."

There it was again. His name. I was trying to ignore it all. I was working not to think about him. But it seemed his name was always there, waiting to be said. What was worse was that Fallon and Tatiana seemed to know why, and I despised it. I didn't like that I had a reason to assist here, even if it was a self-imposed one. I could have just gone home. I didn't have to stay and help. I shouldn't want to help Sayer. Especially not now that it appeared like he knew what Glinda was planning. I really loathed that I was wondering if Glinda had set that up, if she'd made him get close to me, used him to manipulate me, and I hated that I missed him even more. Everything felt out of my control, and I felt like I was being manipulated with little to no information, based on everyone's whims and expectations.

Tatiana and Fallon exchanged a tense look, and with a sad tone to her voice, answered, "Sayer has no choice. He must carry out his orders, most of them anyway, or risk his head. He was never asked to place himself in her service. He did that on his own. He went so Bree would not. He went—"

Fallon put his bowl down on top of his plate quite loudly, causing her to pause. She gave him an apologetic look then continued, "Sayer has done a lot of things, some of them unpleasant, in his attempts to help the people of Oz. Bringing you here would not have been easy for him, but the alternative would have cost him far more. Glinda does not tolerate defiance from her staff."

I nodded, remembering what he'd said when we were traveling here. He had tried to find an alternative, a way to avoid bringing me here altogether, but there hadn't been a choice. He didn't have any choices with Glinda. The few snatched moments we'd had in spite of her had been a risk, but he'd taken them regardless. He'd helped me, loved me, briefly.

I cleared my throat and looked to Fallon. The way he reacted to Glinda when she visited was awful, but he seemed perfectly comfortable with Tatiana. He got along well enough with the monkeys, despite how they'd been behaving. He trusted Sayer. I didn't have the reasons, but he appeared to know these people well enough to judge their character. With no better option, I made the decision there and then to trust his judgment. "Fine. If he can risk his neck, so can I. What happens here while I'm gone? I mean, what if she turns up? Are you going to handle her?"

He folded his arms and sat back in his chair, brows raised.

"You can't come with me, who looks after this place?" I questioned, forgetting all about our guest.

He shrugged and pointed up. Let the monkeys handle it.

"I don't imagine Glinda launching a full-scale attack on her *friend*," Tatiana interjected. Her emphasis on the word 'friend' didn't escape my notice. "She wants you to head east, does she not?"

I tilted my head. "Why does she want me to do that?"

Tatiana smiled. "Because she's gathering her allies."

"What allies?" I asked, brows pulled in. "In preparation for what?"

"War."

The word hung in the air.

Glinda wanted me to fight for her. To take over for her. And then what? I didn't believe she wanted me to be her friend, nor did she want me to restore order to her world for her people. No. I was a small pawn in her big plan to defeat her sister, that was becoming clear. But the sister Glinda wanted me to help her destroy was sitting at my table and treating me as an equal. She was open, and honest, and... nice. Fallon seemed perfectly at ease with her now, which spoke volumes. Remi had come home unscathed after venturing into her territory on my orders. But was that more strategic game playing?

The more questions I asked myself, the harder it was becoming to make a decision.

I was in a difficult position. While Tatiana gave me no reason not to trust her, the history of their treatment of outsiders wasn't great considering what happened to Great Grandma Dot.

"I'll have to give it some thought," I offered, not wanting to give anything away. "I have a lot to do here, I can't go off making a mess elsewhere when my people are busy burying their dead after the madness I brought here with me and the resulting massacre."

Tatiana looked away and I could see remorse on her face. I knew she had heard my insinuation regarding her last arrival here and the subsequent deaths. "I can only apologize," she said sadly, rising from her seat. "You've had a busy few days, you must be ready for some rest. I'll let you think about it, but please let me know what you decide, and know you're welcome at the Overlook any time." With those parting words, she left.

I let her go, even knowing I'd upset her. Manners be damned, I needed to think.

CHAPTER 2

Fallon was glaring at me.

"What? She killed them, Fallon."

He shrugged.

"She didn't have to kill them."

A few moments silence passed before he got up and started collecting the dirty dishes.

"Leave them," I ordered quietly.

He continued.

I sighed, put some magic behind it, and they were gone. "I don't know if that worked, they could be smashed to pieces in the sink, but I want you to leave them."

He grasped the back of the chair in front of him and looked at the door. He wanted me to hurry after Tatiana, but I knew she wouldn't have left yet, and I still had some time.

"I'll catch up to her, but first, I need to know—do you think she's playing me like Glinda is trying to?"

He gave a stern shake of his head.

"Okay. So, I should go east and handle the tower?"

He nodded once.

I let out a heavy breath and lowered my head. "And Remi can look after this place while we're away?"

He moved so silently I wasn't aware he was at my side until he stroked a hand over my hair. I leaned into him and I closed my eyes, taking comfort in his presence. "How bad is it out there?"

He stroked my hair again, and that told me all I needed to know.

Pushing my chair out, I made to go after my missing guest.

"Wait here," I said. "I'll handle it. Can you think of what we're going to need and write me a list? We only need basics, I don't plan on it taking long."

Not bothering to look at him—I didn't want to see his expression in case it was smug—I made my way out of the building and into the courtyard.

She was standing with her back to me, hands on her hips, and scolding a familiar looking Lioneag. To its credit, it wasn't backing down, clicking its beak at her and flapping its enormous wings so wildly the gravel on the ground was disturbed by the downdraft.

Then it looked at me and tilted its head.

"Hello again," I greeted. "What's going on?"

It clicked its beak, looking from me to Tatiana.

"The two of you are acquainted?" she asked although she didn't sound surprised.

I shrugged. "It saw me when you flew into the Opal Palace, then chased Sayer and I over the border into these lands. It couldn't follow."

Tatiana nodded. "That explains a lot. She disappeared for five days last week," she murmured, flicking a stern glance at the bird. "No amount of training has tamed her. I hoped, despite her being undersize... never mind."

Why would her size matter? I imagined it would have its advantages in certain situations, but rather than ask more questions, I stepped forward, and examined the bird. "Sayer said this was the creature that scarred his face."

She laughed and the bird lowered its head. "Yes. The last time I met my sister on neutral ground, Sayer approached my stewardess. This one warned him off. It could have been much worse. But that was the first in a string of misdemeanors. I'm afraid she's turning out to be entirely untrainable. I can't keep her when she's so unruly, it'll upset the others. She'll have to return to the colonies in the mountains."

To my surprise, the creature stepped closer to me, distancing herself from her mistress.

Tatiana looked curious. "She seems drawn to you. Maybe you should take her."

I tried not to look horrified. What use was an untrainable bird? Especially one that had been known to attack my allies. The scar on Sayer's face was nasty. I couldn't risk that happening to anyone else. "I don't know how to look after them," I responded quickly. It was true, but that was a weak argument.

Tatiana smirked. "They look after themselves. It would seem she's been determined to get to you since you arrived in Oz. I think she's trying to tell me something."

I frowned. "What's her name?"

Tatiana looked confused. "Name?"

"Doesn't she have one?"

She shook her head. "Not yet. They're named when they complete their training," Tatiana replied. "She hasn't earned one yet."

I frowned, pondering her words. A name was a huge part of your identity. It's who we are. I danced under an alias for safety, and to keep my two identities separate, but that poor bird didn't have one at all. "So everyone around her has a name and she doesn't?"

Tatiana looked at the Lioneag and stepped back to look at her fully. "Is that your problem?"

The bird took a step toward me in answer, opening her beak wide then snapping it shut.

Tatiana's mouth turned down in the corners and she looked at me. "Name her. She's yours," she declared.

On closer inspection, her feathers weren't black, but a very dark blue. They had an oily finish, making them glossy, and the red tips were bright and vibrant in the bright afternoon light.

I don't know why, but she made me think of a friend from high school. She was short and fierce, a definite force to be reckoned with. So much so her mom, a very traditional Indian woman in her fifties, nicknamed her Kali.

Devil.

I had looked into the deity out of curiosity. She was fascinating, representing both wrath and protection, her name literally meaning she who is black. With that said, she was often depicted as a dark blue, holding knives tipped red with dripping blood.

"You look like a Kali," I noted, meeting her black eyes.

Her response was to extend her wings, ruffle her feathers, and scratch at the gravelly floor with her taloned feet.

"I think she's pleased with that," Tatiana commented, smiling. "I'm sure she'll be much happier here with you."

Kali folded her wings back in and stepped closer to me. I tried not to flinch away from the frightening creature, as I said, "I doubt she'll be very happy here at all. There's nothing for her to do."

"There's plenty. Now that she's an ally, she should be

capable of coming and going. She can help Remi with aerial patrols. She will feed herself, all she needs is purpose and somewhere to sleep," Tatiana explained nonchalantly, as if it was an easy, and very done, deal.

Gravel crunched behind me and I turned to see Fallon approaching. Kali didn't react. I found that strange and looked closer at her. "You don't mind Fallon?"

She watched him until he drew level with us, lowering her head as he reached for my hand.

"She's chosen you. She serves you and those you choose to rule at your side, Ella. She will show Fallon the same respect she shows you," Tatiana informed me.

I had questions but didn't voice them. I didn't want to sound self-depreciating by asking why she'd chosen me. Why she'd want to be with me.

She went on, and recommended, "When you head east, leave her here. The people beyond the forest fear the Lioneag, and your first challenge will be to earn their trust."

"How do I make her stay home?"

Tatiana shrugged, using one hand to beckon her mount closer. "I have no idea. You could try using magic to keep her here. But she must not fly over the eastern border. The winged creatures there will attack her."

I nodded. "Now, just to handle Glinda."

"I would suggest keeping up the pretense for as long as possible," she said, mounting her Lioneag. She sat just before its wing joints, positioning her knees on either side of its neck. "While she believes she has you under her control she is less of a threat, but remember, she wants you to take the tower. Once its power has transferred to you, she will try to take it for herself. Her attack will be vicious and sudden, and she will use those close to her against you. Trust no one."

"But Sayer—"

"Will remain in his role as Glinda's steward. He must appear loyal. We need him to remain safe for as long as possible. With that in mind, if there is an altercation you must protect yourself. If he is forced to act against you, disarm him, but try not to kill him," she directed, matter-of-factly.

Kill Sayer? Even the thought of such a thing made me feel sick to my stomach. I couldn't, even if I had to. "I'll send Remi when I have news," I told her, trying to calm the implications of her words from consuming my thoughts.

She shook her head. "I intend to keep watch. I'll come to you when it is safe. I would rather keep my sister in the dark with regard to my involvement for as long as possible."

"Watch? From where?" I questioned, confused.

She smiled. "You have your means and I have mine. I cannot watch you directly, but I can have messages relayed. I can be near the border and assist if necessary, but it's best if Glinda doesn't discover my involvement. Not yet, anyway."

I nodded and stepped back as her Lioneag flexed its wings.

"Thank you, Ellana. And good luck."

I didn't respond and remained outside until the last of her winged guard flew out of sight. Then I turned to Fallon. "We'll leave in the morning," I stated, wanting to get this over with quickly.

He nodded and reached for my hand. I laced my fingers through his and squeezed gently. He smiled, and then let go and turned back to the fortress. I followed more slowly, thinking through everything that had been said, committing it to memory.

CHAPTER 3

I stood outside, ready to depart. The fortress door slammed shut and I turned to see Fallon approaching. He had a pack slung over one shoulder, his quiver and bow over the other, and a short sword and several knives attached to his belt. He'd changed into green, dyed leathers and long boots, with his hair tied neatly back.

"Let me take that," I offered, reaching for the pack. He shook his head.

I shrugged. "Fair enough."

Remi arrived with Daniel. They both bowed, and Remi asked, "Are you certain you wouldn't like one of us to accompany you, my lady?"

I shook my head. "No, Remi, you're needed here. I don't think Glinda will return, but if she does, or if she sends Sayer, tell them I've gone east and will go directly to her when I'm done there."

When I glanced toward the gate, I saw Kali standing there, looking up at the sky and I inquired, "What's wrong with her?"

"I am not sure," Remi replied. "Perhaps she senses the coming storm."

I looked at him and frowned. "What storm?"

He looked east, but his view was hampered by the rocky walls of the volcano sides. "The one that will follow when you claim your right. War, my lady."

I rubbed my left arm, unsure if the chill I felt was in the air or in response to his words. "Maybe we can avoid that," I hedged, hearing the hesitancy in my own voice.

"Perhaps, but it would be prudent to make ready."

I nodded. "Can you...?"

He smiled at me and bowed his head. "Of course." Then he looked directly into my eyes and said, "Ella, be vigilant, the lands between here and the tower are dangerous. The creatures lurking in the forest are not likely to welcome you, and word of your arrival will have traveled by now. You may not be Dorothy, but the resemblance is uncanny, and you are her heir after all. They will not wait to learn the difference."

I nodded and glanced to the gate. "If I don't come back—"

"You mustn't think that way," he interrupted in a stern voice. "You are our best and last hope. Tatiana is brave but she has a fatal flaw. She loves her family"

"How is that a flaw?" I questioned.

"She cannot do what must be done, she cannot conquer her sister. But you, Ella, have no emotional attachment. It is abundantly clear you are, by nature, a gentle soul, and you have good instincts. You have a sense for who is trustworthy. You can work this out for yourself and I have faith in you to do what is right."

"There isn't a damn thing right about war and killing, Remi," I argued, uneasy with the turn in our conversation.

"No. There isn't. And that is why you're the best hope we have against Glinda's tyranny," Remi warned.

I looked up at the sky to see a patrol of guards fly over. "She seems so harmless, annoying, but harmless. All the frills and the dainty tiaras, tottering around in those little heels." I'd seen through it, more as a result of too many years dealing with other people's bullshit, but the statement still held true.

"I think you can appreciate appearances count for very little."

I looked down at the ground. "She didn't mean to kill the witches, you know. The first, the witch from the east, was in the wrong place at the wrong time. Like, under a house... the second..." I glanced up at the tower where the crystal ball was and sighed. "Well, that was water. Who would have thought she would react like that to water?"

"The green skin should have given that away," he muttered.

I snorted with laughter. I hadn't heard him make a joke before, however dry. "I didn't think of it like that."

He smiled then assured, "Your people here are behind you. When the time comes we will fight for our freedom."

"While I appreciate the sentiment, Remi, I think I'll try to avoid it. I mean, if I know she's going to try to take my head off the minute I do whatever it is I have to do there, then I can stop her. Can't I?"

"She won't do it herself," Daniel cut in. I'd forgotten he was there, he'd been so quiet.

"You don't think she'll... no, he wouldn't," I insisted, shaking my head. Sayer wouldn't hurt me. Would he?

Daniel shrugged. "She'll have something planned and we can't be certain her steward is entirely on our side. Keep Fallon close."

Remi gave him a warning look and he turned away.

I thought for a minute. Daniel was right. Nobody knew anything for certain. Except that Glinda was nuts, which went without saying. But Sayer? He was bound by his vows. I didn't know the full extent of what that meant for him, but I knew his life was on the line if he messed up. He was walking a very fine line.

"If anything bad does happen, I want you to take everyone from here and fly north," I ordered, looking back up at the volcano rim, and wondering how long it would take to reach the border, then how long through the forest.

"Lady?" Remi said, questioning.

"If she does..." I swallowed, not wanting to say it out loud. "Well, if I don't come back I want you all to be safe. Or as safe as you can be. Take everyone without a pair of wings and get away. Tatiana may not be able to protect you, but you have a better chance if you're all together."

"You will come back," Daniel declared with certainty. "You'll come back, we'll face her together, and this war will end."

I frowned, thinking about his words. "When was the last time the two sides fought?"

"It's been eight years," Remi answered. "Our years. Considerably longer in your world. But Glinda hasn't given up. I heard murmurs of growing forces in the south. Of interference with the Wyrms of the northeast. There has been unrest among the Wyrms and the Lioneag for several years. It is assumed the good witch is behind it."

"She's got the... what's a Wyrm?"

"Dragons," Daniel replied. "Well, they're more like winged serpents. With the ability to change color, they're swift and deadly. They're on top of you before you know they're coming. The Lioneag can defend well enough against them, but no one ever knows when they're going to attack. Or where."

I loud screech came from the skies above and I looked up to see two of the guard patrol hovering high above. "What's wrong?"

"I sent them to look ahead. All clear," Remi translated, reading the hand signals one of the patrol were using to relay his message. "You'll have an easy journey from here to the border."

I nodded. We were ready to go, but I had something on my mind. "Remi, your females... women I mean, do they guard too?"

He looked at me, the thick ridge of skin forming his brow crumpling slightly. "Not usually, no."

I nodded. "Do they want to?"

"They've never been asked," he admitted. "We generally keep the women and children away from such... unpleasantness."

"Do me a favor. Ask them. Any who want to defend themselves should be shown how. Arm them. I don't want anyone left helpless," I commanded. I said things would be different and I meant it. Giving everyone a choice wasn't something they have had before.

He bowed his head and I glanced at Daniel. His expression was somewhere between shock and awe. "What?" I asked.

He shook his head. "Nothing, my lady."

"There's something."

Remi cleared his throat. "I think Daniel is surprised at your consideration. The women are often forgotten."

I cry above drew my attention, and I looked up as Kali flew into the basin of the volcano and circled the fortress before landing close to me.

"We can't afford that," I called over my shoulder to Remi, walking toward Kali. "And this was all started by a woman. It's only fair that those of us who aren't power crazed, balls of cotton candy represent themselves against her. That goes for everyone. Every citizen should be equipped to defend themselves. Send someone down to the village, relay the same message to the Pumpkinheads. If this is going to turn nasty, I want everyone here to have a chance of survival."

Both guards bowed and I turned to Fallon. "Ready?"

He smiled at me then glanced to Remi. A look passed between them, and then Fallon gave a stern nod and turned to look toward the gates.

"Be careful, Ella," Remi called as Fallon set off walking.

I nodded. "You too. I'll see you soon."

He bowed and I turned to Kali. She spread her wings and took to the sky, and I set off after her, following Fallon up the gravel pathway to the gates.

CHAPTER 4

Wearing my leggings, a baggy tee, and my glittering, magical converse sneakers, I followed Fallon through the fields forming my lands. Some were green, whatever crops planted there apparently growing well, while others were the telltale gold of ripe corn ready to be harvested. That was all I could see for miles ahead. There were no signs of anyone tending the fields. No signs of anything but a few butterflies dancing over the tops of the plants around us.

Behind us, the volcano sat like a black growth on the otherwise perfect landscape. I could see the aerial patrols coming and going from the fortress as my people looked for threats, prepared to defend their home against whatever foe may come too close.

"Glinda won't just turn up, will she?" I asked Fallon.

He slowed, then turned to face me. I still wasn't used to seeing him, or anyone, so well armed. Not in reality. I'd seen all the usual movies, the ranger in his supple leather armor, lurking in shadows and fighting bad guys, but having that right here in front of me was a strange experience. His hair was pulled back from his face and a few days growth formed a light beard along his jawline. The scent of leather was prominent when I got too close, and when he moved, there was the sound of arrows rustling in his quiver and the light squeak of his boots. He was every bit the rugged hunter from my favorite shows, and when he looked at me, I remembered who he was out of the armor.

Brushing a few stray strands of hair back from my face, he shook his head.

"I mean, I know I'm not much against her," I began, worried for the people now under my protection, "but if she came and hurt anyone—"

His thumb brushed my bottom lip, cutting me off, and it was all I could do not to part my lips and draw it into my mouth.

My blood heated in my veins at the simple gesture and my breath hitched.

The option was there to take full advantage of the situation. Him. Me. No one to be seen for miles. It was tempting, and he moved a fraction of an inch closer as Kali swooped overhead, breaking the moment.

She didn't seem to be warning him, but he took my right hand, turned abruptly, and set off walking east.

Smiling to myself, I allowed him to lead me toward our destination. He was probably right to let the moment pass. We didn't have time. I needed to stay a step ahead of Glinda, and I wasn't going to achieve that by rolling around in cornfields.

We walked all day, eating lunch on the move, and in the late afternoon I noticed there was a clear change in the landscape. The fields ended abruptly, barred by what appeared to be a forest.

"Are we here already?" I asked.

Fallon shook his head and smiled.

"If this isn't the western border, where are we?"

He pointed to his left.

"North?"

He nodded, then pointed directly ahead.

"Oh," I responded, beginning to understand. "We have to cut though here to reach the east. This is Tatiana's territory?"

He nodded again and shifted the bag on his back before taking my hand.

"Oh, well at least the dangerous parts don't start right away," I quipped, lacing my fingers through his and stepping toward the ominous looking forest.

Kali landed behind me, snapping her beak, and I paused before turning back to her. "Sorry... Umm, you need to go back to the fortress," I hesitantly told her. She still made me nervous.

She pulled back her head and blinked. Having to constantly figure out what facial expressions and gestures meant was exhausting, and I sighed before explaining, "Look, this may be Tatiana's land, but I can't risk anything happening to you. She handed you over to me and expects you to be looked after. She said to keep you in my lands and that's what I intend to do. Please, Kali. Go back to the fortress, help Remi keep lookout. Any visitors aren't welcome until I get back, okay?"

She snapped her beak again and scratched the ground with one of her huge, clawed feet, but didn't protest. Then she spread her wings.

"Thank you. Be good, we'll be there and back in no time. Promise," I assured her, letting out a relieved breath that she wasn't going to fight me on this.

I watched her fly away then turned back to set off walking, and murmured, "Okay, nice leisurely stroll through the forest."

Fallon pulled me back and I turned to see him shaking his head.

I rolled my eyes. "Of course I know it's dangerous. Don't tell me, lions and tigers?"

He looked at me as though he were surprised I'd know anything at all.

"Grandma Dot's book," I stated, stepping forward. "She met that lion, didn't she? And the woodcutter, and the scarecrow. Maybe we'll make some new friends along the way."

I looked around and noticed the landscape changed slightly a little farther north. "Aren't we taking the road?"

His reply was a tug forward as he began to walk, not to the road but toward the forest. I didn't question him, gazing down to see we were already on a small dirt track, and let him lead me under the cover of the trees. I realized my sneakers would end up filthy on the muddy trail and changed them to Doc Martens. They were much better for walking through muddy, creepy woods, even if the glorious red garnet stood out against the miserable browns of the tree trunks and mud.

After the trees I'd seen in the south, these seemed far more natural, if a bit creepy. No fancy topiary, just gnarly branches with a few browning leaves clinging on pitifully. Strangely, there was no sign of fallen leaves on the ground.

We walked for what seemed like hours, forced to amble single file along the increasingly narrowing trail with me in the lead, when the trees began to thin out on our right.

"What's over there?" I inquired, slowing down.

Fallon stopped. I turned back to look at him and didn't like his expression. It was the same look of sadness everyone seemed to wear when they mentioned the city.

"The city?"

He nodded, and I turned to head through the trees toward the city.

Before I could move anywhere he reached for me, taking me by the shoulder and halting my movements. "What? I only want to peek. Satisfy my morbid curiosity," I explained.

He sighed and followed my lead as I picked my way through the forest.

The wood ended abruptly, the muddy ground changing to an arid, black dust.

"What the hell went on here? I thought it was just a figure of speech when they said the place burned." I couldn't hide the shock in my voice. The image before me was beyond comprehension.

Fallon didn't say anything, and following the tree line, I moved around the outskirts of the city.

The place was a mess. Tumbled remains of buildings and burned out shells of smaller dwellings, like the ones I'd stayed in back east when I was on my way to the fortress, littered the ground.

"I want to get closer," I murmured, looking to Fallon.

He shook his head and I veered right, determined to get a better look.

He grasped my wrist.

"What?"

He shook his head again.

"Why? If it's a ruin, what could be there that could hurt us?"

Lips pressed into a firm line, he gave me a stern look

I pouted. "Fine. I want to see the place soon though. If I'm going to do this, I need to know what I'm dealing with," I capitulated.

He released my wrist and dropped his shoulders, stepping around me and heading toward the edge of the wood. So, pouting worked on Fallon? Good to know.

I followed, trying not to look smug and carefully stepping through the ruins.

The light was fading, but the destruction was clearly visible. The tallest structure sat in the center, and I assumed it was the palace or whatever they'd called it, with its jagged walls reaching for the sky. They didn't reach as far as they used to, that was clear. And it wasn't made of emerald as my great grandmother's story had claimed. It looked black from where I stood. Black and broken and just miserable.

I turned to Fallon and noticed he was looking out at the city with sadness etched on his face. "What happened?"

His lips parted as though he was going to say something, but he took a breath and lowered his head.

"Glinda and Tatiana?" I prompted.

He sighed before looking up, and I reached out to touch his arm.

"I'm sorry. It must be frustrating when I keep asking questions you can't answer."

Taking my hand, he pulled me toward him and reached for my face with his free hand.

I smiled, leaning into his palm, and he bent his head to kiss me.

There was always so much said in his kiss, in this case, I was certain he meant for me not to apologize. That it didn't matter that he couldn't answer verbally. That we'd manage just fine. And it amazed me how well we could communicate despite him being mute.

It's getting dark," I said as he pulled away. "Are we going to find somewhere to rest for the night?"

He looked south to the ruined city, and he seemed to be searching for something.

Not finding whatever it was he was looking for, he turned and headed back toward the trees. I followed, happy to leave that miserable place behind me for the time being.

Back under cover of the forest, Fallon walked with more purpose.

After a while, I interrupted the silence. "I don't really want to be stumbling through a forest in the dark. Is there somewhere we can rest?"

He took a heavy breath in and looked around, then presented his hand, palm up.

"Here? What if it rains?"

He curled his hand into a fist, but left his index finger out, pointing up and drawing a circle with the tip of his finger.

I rolled my eyes. "You want me to come up with something? Isn't this taking advantage of my ability or something?"

He smirked and sat down cross-legged, apparently prepared to wait.

"Fine," I gave in, turning my back on him and looking at the space around us. We were in a small clearing. There was space for a small structure, but I'd never created anything from nothing before. The fortress was more of a repair job, and the defensive barriers I'd placed around my lands weren't a building. It was difficult to describe precisely how that occurred, but it wasn't the same.

I concentrated on the empty space, trying to think of something small but sturdy enough to house us. The best I could come up with was a copy of the small wooden houses the Pumpkinheads lived in.

I turned to Fallon as the structure popped into existence, and inquired, "Will that do?"

He got to his feet and gave me an impressed nod of his head.

"Suppose it'll come in handy for the way back," I commented, as he strode forward and tugged on the door.

It swung open and he glanced inside before holding out his hand.

"Did you bring dinner or shall I attempt to handle that too?" I teased, smirking at him.

He shoved the small of my back as I passed and I laughed.

"I'm joking!"

I had managed to create the basics. There was a bed, a small wood burning stove, and a table complete with plates, spoons, and a frying pan, and I flopped down onto the bed with a sigh, weary from our journey.

Fallon dropped his bag on the floor and sat beside me, looking around the single room.

"So far so good," I noted.

He turned and looked at me with his brows pulled in.

"I mean, we haven't run into any trouble. Yet."

He raised his brows twice in quick succession and smirked.

"Maybe we'll make it there without any?" I could only hope.

He lay on his back at my side and sighed.

"I wish I knew why you couldn't speak," I said, reaching for his hand. "I know Glinda did it, but how? Why?"

He glanced my way, lacing his fingers through mine.

Then it dawned on me. His behavior around her. His trust in Sayer. His determination to help me. Holy shit.

"Did you turn her down?"

He nodded.

Rage burned in the pit of my stomach. She took his voice

because he went against her wishes? Who did that? I knew her kind and gentle persona was an act. The woman was a complete psychopath. Sociopath? Whatever, she was nuts. But she didn't know I was on to her. "She wanted you as her steward?"

He nodded again.

"As well as Sayer?"

His eyes met mine.

"Is he screwing her?" I snarled, unable to keep the rage out of my tone.

He shook his head and released my hand to stroke my cheek.

"Nice," I said, with a humorless laugh. "Just me then."

He sat up, took my face in both hands, and kissed me, then placed his right hand over my chest.

I laughed. "He doesn't love me."

He pressed his lips together and smiled, then moved his hand from my chest to his and back again. He loved me. They loved me?

"Why?"

Turning his lips down in the corners, he tilted his head and reached for my face.

"Don't tell me I'm beautiful. That isn't a reason to love someone," I chided. I wanted someone to want me for me, not my looks, since that always seemed to be what drew men's attention.

I got up from the bed and moved toward the door.

He followed, taking my hand and spinning me to face him. There was a look of frustration in his eyes. I gave him a questioning look and tugged my hand free as he backed me against the wall, grasping my wrists and raising them over my head.

Unable to tell me anything, he lost control before he

could communicate any further and kissed me. It was hard, desperate. I felt his frustration at not being able to convey his message in any other way than the firm grip he had on my wrists and the way his body pressed into mine.

I'd never seen the forceful side of him, and I liked it. I groaned into his mouth as he forced my lips open with his own, his tongue meeting mine and making his point. He'd never kissed me like this, no one had ever kissed me like this, and I felt my need for him throb. Rather than press my thighs together, I raised my knee and settled it on his hip as his mouth claimed mine. He ground his hips against me, and I tilted my hips to better feel his hard cock beneath his pants.

He took the hint. Transferring his grasp on my wrists to hold them with just one hand, he traced one finger down the side of my face to my throat. I felt his fingers twitch, his thumb pressing into to the hollow, before moving on. The way he squeezed my breast made me gasp, and he responded with a hard pinch to my nipple. The pain increased my need, and I hooked my foot around the back of his thigh, forcing him closer.

I almost sobbed when he slid his hand into my pants, moaning when his flinger slid between my lips and found me slick with need for him. Pulling away, he held my gaze and retracted his hand, bringing his finger up to my mouth. He watched me suck itclean, his brown eyes alight.

I couldn't have spoken if I'd wanted to, but my lips twitched up at one side at his expression. Then his hands were on my waist, turning me to face the wall, and tugging my ass back toward him. I wiggled my hips as he tugged down my pants and underwear, exposing me to him, and braced my hands against the wall as he thrust inside. He fucked me hard, wrapping his hand around the length of my hair and pulling my head back onto his shoulder to make my back arch further. The angle, the discomfort, the pain of him tugging at my hair with every thrust pushed me to orgasm faster than he was expecting, and I heard him suck in a breath as I pulsed around his cock. I wanted to press against him further, to grind against him and squeeze every last sensation out of it, but he held me firm and kept pounding. He wasn't far behind, and pulled me into him so he could kiss my shoulder as he inched toward his own release. The kiss built and turned into a bite as he forced himself deeper, and I hissed through my teeth. He released me at once, hair and neck, and pulled me close.

Panting, I suggested, "We should probably get some sleep."

His arm tightened around my waist and he kissed my neck, then pulled my panties up for me. I kicked off my boots and stepped out of my pants, allowing him to lead me to bed.

Okay. There was far more to it than him thinking I was beautiful. He couldn't put it into words, and that was okay. He trusted me almost immediately when I'd done nothing to earn it. He'd already done so much for me, and had shown me without words that he cared. I could do the same for him.

CHAPTER 5

We ate breakfast quickly and left just after daybreak. Fallon seemed eager to get moving and he set off at a faster pace than he'd walked the previous day.

It was cold and still dark, with a heavy mist creeping through the trees, giving the place an even more ominous feel. I'd dressed myself in jeans, a tank top and a plaid shirt to keep me warmer as we walked.

He headed northeast for a while, before turning and heading directly east. It surprised me that I knew what direction we were moving in, but I shrugged it off as another weird side effect of the powers I'd inherited.

"Is it just me, or are these getting creepier?" I asked, gesturing toward the trees as they became denser. It was clear we were entering an older part of the forest. The trees were taller, their trunks thicker and more gnarled the farther we walked. "And it's so quiet, it's weird. The only sound here is the occasional snapping of twigs. And do you get the feeling you're being watched? It's probably just me... Fallon?"

He'd paused a few paces ahead and held up a hand.

I stopped. "What?"

Without communicating anything to me, he removed his bow from his shoulder and drew an arrow from the quiver on his back.

I turned around, looking back the way we came. I couldn't see much, the morning mist still hadn't cleared, and all I could hear was my own pulse in my ears. I turned forward, and saw the same mist. The same trees.

"There's nothing there," I said in a loud whisper.

Fallon backed toward me, his footsteps almost silent, then loosed an arrow off to my right.

I looked in that direction and thought I saw a shadow moving through the trees, but it was hard to tell in the half light and dispersing mist.

"What was that?" I whispered, suddenly afraid.

Fallon hissed, nocking another arrow.

The eerie silence was broken by a low, guttural growl. It was hard to describe the sound, but I was sure I'd heard it somewhere before.

Fallon grasped my shoulder and stepped around me, aiming his arrow in the direction of the sound.

Whether he heard it, I wasn't sure, but there was a sound behind me, and I turned slowly, holding my breath. I didn't really want to know what was there. I wanted to run screaming, but I was frozen as I looked directly into a pair of gleaming, black lined, amber eyes.

It took me a second to realize what I was looking at, but as my eyes slid over his thick muzzle, broad forehead and thick, black mane, my heart stuttered in my chest.

"Fallon, put the bow down..."

He spun so quickly he almost knocked me off balance, and I had to throw out an arm to steady myself.

My sudden movement spurred the creature into action, and my stomach clenched so hard I thought I would vomit as Fallon pushed me aside.

I collided with the thick trunk of the closest tree, and my hands slipped on the light coating of damp moss, grazing my palms and causing me to stumble.

I righted myself and turned to see where Fallon was as the lion charged past.

I'd never seen one outside of a zoo, and certainly never with enough room to run free. Of course, I had watched the occasional wildlife documentary while dying from alcohol poisoning on my sofa on Sundays, but even then you didn't get the magnificent scale of the damn things. Despite his size he was nimble, and I watched in horror as he turned to charge again.

But he wasn't running at me. He was heading directly for Fallon. His mouth was open, displaying his sharp canines, and his eyes were narrowed as he focused on his prey.

Fallon was already prepared, an arrow nocked and aimed, and he fired directly at it.

The lion stumbled, tripping over its huge paws, and fell at Fallon's feet.

"Fallon, no!" I yelled, as he dropped the bow and reached for the sword at his hip. "Don't."

The lion moaned and I stepped forward to inspect it. The poor thing was only acting on its instincts. Protecting its home against intruders. The monkeys had done precisely the same thing when Tatiana came, and had died for it. There'd been enough death. Enough killing.

The arrow was lodged in its shoulder, and it was clearly in pain. "Fallon, I don't think it was trying to kill us. It was protecting its home. You can't kill it."

Fallon didn't need to be able to speak to communicate

his feelings. It was all there, clearly etched on his face. It had attacked me, and he was going to repay it in kind.

"Do not kill that lion," I ordered more forcefully.

He stayed his hand and looked at me.

"I mean it. We can't go slaughtering our way through this. We need to get that arrow out and let it go."

Sword in his right hand, he gestured at the lion, then me with his left.

"It's a lion, it's what they do."

He rolled his eyes and jabbed the point of his sword in the beast's side. It didn't move.

"Leave it alone," I said, stepping forward.

It was clearly in pain, but still managed a ferocious snarl as I crouched at its side.

"If you stay still, I can help." I don't know why I was surprised it seemed to understand me. "Please," I begged, reaching for the arrow, "let me help you."

I glanced up at Fallon. The look of exasperation on his face was enough, but the way he shook his head at me, stepping back slightly, didn't put me off. I glanced back down at the Lion.

"I'm going to pull it out, I need you to stay very still and keep those teeth to yourself."

It puffed out a breath, closed its eyes, and I saw its body tense as I reached for the arrow.

Fallon touched my shoulder and I gazed up at him. His eyes were full of caution.

"I have to."

I gripped the shaft of the arrow tightly and pulled. It was deeply embedded in the muscle, and I felt it release with a sickening gush of blood. I quickly pressed my free hand down on the wound, his warm blood coating my palm. I needed gauze or something to soak up the blood, and squeezed my eyes shut, willing something to appear.

"Keep still," I murmured, as a thick wad of clean cloth formed between my hand and the lion, and I leaned down hard. "I know it hurts. The bleeding should—"

It happened so fast there wasn't time for me to get out of the way. The lion rolled, pushing me back, and was on its feet in an instant. I lost my balance and sprawled on the ground, looking up at the massive creature with wide eyes.

It snarled at Fallon then turned to me, its mouth wide as it roared in my face. The sound was deafening, but rather than turn away, I stared directly into its open mouth.

His teeth were sharp and unnaturally white.

"Please don't..." I was distracted by movement on my left and saw Fallon had an arrow pointed directly at the side of the lion's head. "Fallon, no!"

He ignored me, and I noticed the lion glance in his direction.

"Please... Fallon, don't hurt him." I turned toward the lion, and pleaded, "Look, I know what you're thinking. Please don't kill me. I know you can understand what I'm saying. I'm not asking you to trust me, just let me explain before this gets out of hand. Please."

His lips twitched, bringing my focus back to his jaws, and I was certain he was just going to eat me anyway. But if he did, Fallon would attack him, and if he wasn't fast enough then the lion would probably kill him too.

"I'm not what you think," I began, holding out my hands. "I'm not Dorothy. I'm trying to help."

Fallon had stepped back, pulling the string of his bow taut, the arrow ready to pierce the side of the lion's head—a kill shot.

"Fallon, don't... I'm Ella, I'm working with Glinda—"

The lion snarled again, swiping at me with a massive paw. I flinched to the side.

"Wait, I'm not her ally... she's using me. My great grandmother killed the Witches of the East and West, their power transferred to me, but to use it effectively I have to take over the castles. She wants me to take the East. Then, I think she's going to try to kill me. I don't want that. I don't even want to be here, but I can't go home until I've done what has to be done. I have no intention of handing power to her or anyone else. I don't even want it for myself. I just want to put things right and go back to Kansas."

The lion turned its head and roared at Fallon, warning him to back up. I was relieved when he took the hint.

"I'm trying to help," I continued, drawing its attention back to me. "Please."

It stepped closer to me, and I considered trying to back away, but there was nowhere to go and no time to get out of its way. Instead, I leaned my head back and sighed.

"If you kill me, Glinda could take everything. East. West. The city. Tatiana won't stand a chance. If you kill Fallon, then that's one more person trying to help taken out. If you kill the people working against Glinda, you condemn everyone to living at her mercy. Please..."

Fallon had moved so he was standing a few feet from my head. I could just make him out, and hoped he'd lowered the bow.

"Please," I whispered, closing my eyes.

I couldn't say anything more. He either believed me or he didn't. Or I'd been talking to a wild animal that had no idea what I was saying, and it was going to kill me regardless of who I was or why I was there. In which case, I had to get Fallon away.

"Fallon," I called quietly. "Run."

I opened my eyes about to kick the thing in the chest, but it was gone. In its place stood a man with black, braided hair and deep bronze skin. His thick brows framed a pair of amber eyes that glared down at me with no small amount of disgust. His full lips parted, and the top lip lifted in a sneer as he glanced up at Fallon and barked, "Who is she?"

I rolled over into my stomach and looked at Fallon as I pushed myself up from the ground. "*She* is Ellana Rose," I answered, turning to face him, "the heir of Dorothy, like I said."

His shoulder was still bleeding, but it seemed to be clotting without pressure on the wound, and I looked over the rest of him. His muscled chest was bare, with a thick mat of black hair covering most of his skin. He was large in build, easily a hundred pounds heavier than Fallon, and more muscular. He wore what appeared to be linen shorts, thankfully, and was barefoot. His thighs were thick, his shorts tight, and his calves bulged he was so well toned. He was as close to physically perfect as a man could get, but I wasn't letting that sway me. Not this time. I'd made enough assumptions based on appearance.

"What are you doing in Tatiana's lands?" he snarled.

"Passing through, with her permission," I informed him, dusting myself off. Some of the dirt was very wet and clung to my pants. I gave up on it after a few swipes and looked up at him. "I claimed the West and the forces there. Then we were escorted to the border by a Lioneag, who Tatiana gave me, and plan to travel east on foot. As I said, I'm expected to take control of the Quartz Tower."

His eyes narrowed and he pursed his full lips. "And the Witch of the North knows all of this?" He didn't sound convinced.

I nodded. "She visited me yesterday, we discussed the options, this is the only way."

He glanced at Fallon and I looked back to see him nod his confirmation.

"If you have the power of the west, why did you not defend yourself?" he demanded. "How are we to know you aren't manipulating us?"

I sighed. "Because I'm not here to kill everyone. I don't want to make enemies, I just want to... well, apparently I'm the best chance to stop that psychotic pink pompom from taking over. She manipulated my great grandma, but she can't manipulate me. I know what she did. I want to put things right. My grandma was just a kid and Glinda exploited her. She made her kill for her. It destroyed her life."

"So you want revenge?" he prompted, cocking his head.

I shook mine. "No. Not revenge. That won't help anyone. I just want to undo some of the damage. It won't bring back all the people who died, and it won't fix the mess it made of my grandmother's life, but it might just clear my family name and stop Glinda from doing whatever it is she plans to do when she takes over."

Apparently done listening to our exchange, Fallon moved around me and picked up the pack he'd dropped while trying to fend off the lion. Then he took me by the hand and stepped forward.

The man stepped aside, letting us pass, and inquired, "How do the people know they can trust you?"

"They don't," I retorted, not looking back. "Just as I didn't know you wouldn't kill me. But that didn't stop me from telling Fallon not to hurt you. Believe me or don't, but I have to go. The sooner I reach the tower, the sooner this is over."

"It isn't so simple," he called as I set off walking again. Fallon fell behind, shielding me from the shapeshifter.

I didn't respond. I didn't have time. I needed to reach the East before Glinda discovered I was heading there. With the power of the two kingdoms, I had a chance to defend myself. That was my hope anyway.

We hadn't gone far when the sound of twigs snapping came from ahead. I didn't slow down. I didn't react at all when the lion man stepped out into my path from between two very large trees.

"Okay. What isn't simple?" I questioned, as I stepped around him.

Fallon had stopped. I turned around to see the shapeshifter staring me down.

"Look, I know I look like a Dorothy. I know the people here have no reason to trust me. But I also know that there are three of us with magical powers and one tower that needs me to claim ownership if I'm to help return this place to any sort of normality." I pointed south. "That city is ruined. I know what it was like before the two sisters burned it down fighting. I've read all about it. I've seen the destruction. I've seen the people of the West fighting with their allies from the North. I've seen *my* people die to defend their home and me in it. I won't pretend to have the answers, but I can't sit back and allow more innocent lives be lost because one lunatic wants to rule it all. I didn't ask to come here anymore than Dorothy did. Glinda brought us both. We're both pawns to her. The people here don't matter to her, all she wants is more and more power. I'm not the bad guy. I'm trying to help," I concluded with a huff, just wanting to get to the tower.

The lion didn't move, but he did make an odd, "pfft pfft"

sound that didn't sound at all threatening. It seemed more peaceful. Accepting.

I looked at Fallon who lowered his head.

"Okay," I mumbled, running my hands over my head to smooth down my hair. "So, I'm moving east. Come with me, or don't. Believe me, or don't, but there isn't time to stand around pleading my case. I need that tower. The people need me, whether they accept me or not."

I turned my back on him and started to move. I didn't know where I was going, the trail long since having blended in with the dirt, so I continued in as straight a line and hoped Fallon had followed.

CHAPTER 6

The morning passed in silence as we trudged through the miserable waste of a forest. Fallon had insisted we stop once, at what I assumed to be noon, to eat. We sat on a fallen tree trunk and I picked at some bread, cheese, and apples, while the lion watched us from a few feet away. Fallon offered him some, I assumed as a peace offering as much as out of hospitality, but he didn't shift back into human form.

Fallon had shrugged and returned the food to his pack, and we resumed our journey after allowing the food to settle in our stomachs.

We'd been walking for a while, with the lion following behind me, when I addressed Fallon, "Do you think I'll have the same reception when we get to... wherever we're going?"

He slowed, allowing me to catch up to him, then stopped. He shrugged in response, then gave me a smile that I took to mean 'I hope not.'

"They have no reason to trust me though," I pondered, voicing my thoughts to the silent man. "It doesn't really matter what I tell them. I'm just another outsider coming to cause problems. Even if we had Sayer here, another voice on my side to plead my case, it'd be difficult."

He cupped my face in his right hand and kissed me gently. I smiled, tucking my hair behind my ear, and glanced to my left. The lion had sat down and was watching us. I couldn't make out his expression. So far, I'd worked out going to rip my face off and not going to rip my face off, and that was about it.

Feeling self-conscious from his stare, I turned and started walking again.

* * *

WE DIDN'T STOP until nightfall. The forest hadn't changed at all, but a path had opened up and we followed it without hindrance. It was just miserable. Everything about it was. No grass. No flowers. No wildlife. It made me miss the clear skies and yellow fields surrounding the fortress, and even the lush green of the South. Mostly, though, I began to miss home. I'd managed to put it out of my mind until then, but with nothing to distract me, my thoughts returned to Kansas. To the open landscape. The people who I'd come to love, my acquaintances at work and the dusty old house I was supposed to be fixing up. I'd spent my entire life there, and I'd just become the next generation to take on Gale Farm. That was where I belonged, not here, risking my life for a bunch of people who either didn't trust me or wanted to kill me on sight.

With the lion man accompanying us, I thought better of creating somewhere to sleep, and opted for the heavy blankets Fallon had packed and a fire to keep us warm. Soon after eating, Fallon looked tired and I had to assure him it was safe for him to sleep.

I watched him, focusing on the steady rise and fall of his chest as he slept on his back with one arm behind his head. His sword was held in the other, his bow and quiver beside him, and I sat a few feet away with one of his daggers at my side.

"Was that all true?" the lion man asked, having changed back to his human form.

He was sitting at the opposite side of the fire, still wearing nothing but a pair of shorts. The firelight danced in his eyes as he sat, studying me. I studied right back. He was heavy set, and the strength in his shoulders was clear. His legs were muscular, and despite his size, he looked as though he could cover a great distance in very little time.

His braids hung over his shoulders, deepening the shadows around his face, and intensifying his gaze.

I pulled in my brows, confused. "Was what true?"

"The tale you spun. You did well with a man-eating lion in your face, I admit, but it still doesn't seem entirely likely."

I gave a derisive sniff and looked back to Fallon. "Do you think he'd be helping me otherwise?"

He shrugged and lay on his side, still watching me. "You're a witch."

"Yeah? And what about Sayer? Tatiana? Would one of her Lioneag come to me willingly if I weren't being truthful?"

He rolled onto his back and looked up at the gnarled boughs above us. "Sayer. He's a traitor. He turned his back on us all the second Glinda looked like the safest option. Don't trust him."

I looked away. He'd had to, Tatiana said. He'd done it for them. Hadn't he?

I was close to asking why he was protecting Tatiana's lands if he didn't trust her judgment, but thought better of it.

Her involvement in my plans wasn't common knowledge and we needed to keep it that way if we hoped to stay ahead of Glinda.

"Look," he began, turning onto his side and propping his head in his hand. "If you were in her position, would you go and collect the girl yourself or send a pretty boy to lure her?"

"I wasn't lured," I replied quietly.

"No?"

I was kidnapped, I thought to myself. Sayer hadn't given me a choice, but I knew now he hadn't had one either. I didn't blame him. This was all on her. "No."

"So you're here by choice?" he pressed.

"Right now, I'm choosing to try and prevent any more cities from being burned to the ground," I countered, locking eyes with him. "By choice. And if you can't help with that, I see no point in you being here."

"I have people to protect," he argued.

"I appreciate that, but going around slaughtering anyone who steps into the forest won't help you keep your family safe."

He looked away and I mentally chastised myself. His family was probably dead, along with however many millions that got caught up in that ridiculous war.

"I'm sorry," I said quietly. "I didn't think..."

He sighed. "There are very few of us left. She tricked my people into peace talks, then set her traitorous steward to work. We were never a large race, never reaching more than a few hundred in number, and she got them all together in one place and destroyed them. But—"

"He tried to save people, and he's branded a traitor?" I snapped, cutting him off.

He huffed a small laugh. "Is that what he told you? Far

be it for me to tell you otherwise, if that's what he has you believing."

I looked at him and he looked at me. His expression wasn't hostile, more apologetic. As though he wasn't happy to be delivering more unpleasant versions of events.

"But, as I was saying," he continued after a moment's pause, "I refused to go. I'm all that's left, and I joined the other species who went into hiding. We worked to hide others, saving as many as we could. Slaughtering anyone who steps into the forest does keep them safe."

I understood how they'd drawn that conclusion, but if he had killed me and Fallon, he would have condemned them all to an eternity of living in hiding. "I really am trying to help," I promised, staring into the flames. "My great grandmother was brought here in a tornado. She was only a girl. The house she was in at the time landed on the Witch of the East, killing her. The witch's shoes transferred to her along with the power she possessed, but Dorothy had no idea. Then out of nowhere, a beautiful princess arrived in a bubble and told her she was Glinda the Good. Of course, a young girl in a strange place who'd just accidentally killed someone would believe she was helping her. Of course, she'd do everything she said. The things she saw, the things she did here, tortured her all her life. It made her so ill she was branded insane and locked away. When she finally managed to convince them she was sane, she returned home only to be marginalized. She raised a daughter alone on her family's farm and wrote down what happened in a book.

"Years later, I was born and the stories were told to me, and one night I was brought here to the Opal Palace and told I'm the key to this place's salvation.

"I expect Glinda thought she would get the same

Dorothy back. The difference in time saw two generations in before she managed to get her little soldier back. Only I'm not what she thought she was getting. I'm not an impressionable young girl and I don't trust just anyone. I can usually tell when someone is being deceitful. I can tell when someone is fake. Not long after I arrived here, someone went to great and dangerous lengths to reveal to me what's really going on here, or some of it at least, and earned that trust. I took the power I was asked to claim. I defended the West when it was under attack. I've forged alliances and promised to do my best to help the people here because I've grown up learning all about the person who caused this. I don't blame the people here for being dubious, since the last member of my family to come here was brought to carry out a killing spree, but I'm determined to earn their trust. I intend to deserve it, even if I'm killed for trying."

He lay quietly for a few minutes then got to his feet. "I want to show you something," he informed me, waiting for me to stand.

I frowned before looking at Fallon. He was in a deep sleep and had turned onto his side, still gripping the hilt of his sword. "Is this the part where I follow you a little way into the trees and you slit my throat?"

His mouth twitched with the hint of a smile, but he shook his head. "Nah. Killing you won't help anyone."

He turned and walked away, the darkness swallowing him up.

I remained where I was, not sure what to do. It wasn't safe to leave Fallon alone. It wasn't safe to follow a stranger into the darkness. But if I didn't show him some trust, could I really hope to receive his?

I stood up and tucked the dagger into the waistband of my pants.

"Don't go anywhere," I murmured, stepping around him and following our new friend into the shadows.

He was leaning against the trunk of a tree just a few yards away, and as soon as I reached him, he began to walk.

"I'm Nox," he said after a while.

"Ellana," I responded in kind, stumbling over a tree root, "but my friends call me Ella."

He didn't acknowledge that he'd heard me, and continued to lead me into the dark woods. I could hardly see in the gloom, and wondered how he remembered his way around the forest. I didn't say anything else, assuming he was done with pleasantries.

"Well, away from the trails there are hidden places," he said after a while, not looking back to make sure I was following. "When the city was destroyed the people fled. Most were caught, but some made it far enough into the woods so her forces lost track and gave up. They don't stay in one place for long, for obvious reasons, but Tatiana leaves them alone, and those of us who can help keep them fed."

I wasn't sure he was aware that I knew, but he'd walked us around in a semi-circle, and we were heading back west. I allowed him to lead me, wondering just how deep into the woods he planned for us to go. "And you're telling me this because?"

He stopped walking and looked back at me, his amber eyes gleaming in the dark. That answered my questions regarding how he knew his way around so well. He could actually see. "Got to earn trust, haven't we?"

I frowned and moved to his side. He was almost a foot taller than me, and up close he was scary big, but I looked up and smiled in response, not letting him see any fear.

"I'm going to have to change," he told me. "Wait here, I'll

let them know I've brought a visitor, and come back. I won't be long."

Before I could respond he ran off between the trees, not making a sound.

Standing alone in the dark, I chastised myself for being so stupid. Of course he'd left me. He probably set the whole thing up, and some friends of his were waiting to attack Fallon while he lured me into the forest to put a stop to my plans before I could get anywhere near the tower.

Stupid.

I'd kept people at arm's length for years, and when it really mattered how choosy I was with my friends, I'd allowed this to happen.

I was considering trying to retrace my steps when there was a familiar "pfft" sound behind me, and I turned to see a pair of amber eyes gleaming in the murky black of the forest. He turned and stalked back the way he'd apparently come, and despite the doubts in my mind, I followed.

We didn't walk far when I saw a dim light ahead. It quickly grew and I realized it was a small fire.

The trees thinned and opened into a clearing with a small dirt mound off to my left.

Nox approached the fire and lay down, while I remained by the last of the trees, watching. There was a small opening in the mound that looked like a large rabbit hole. Nox seemed perfectly at ease by the fire, and after a few moments a small, furry body darted from the hole in the mound and launched itself at his face.

Nox let out a low rumble and rolled onto his back as another figure, considerably larger than the first, crept from the little den.

Nox sat up and looked over at me, then looked at the newcomer and dipped his head.

It appeared to be enough of a sign that I wasn't a threat, so the figure drew up on his hind legs and walked into the firelight.

He was around three feet tall and hairy. His ears lay flat against his head as he surveyed me, I assumed calculating the risk.

The smaller creature continued its assault on Nox, biting at his ears and scrambling over his head.

"Hello," I said, taking a tentative step forward. "I'm Ella."

The adult creature turned sharply toward Nox, his thick bushy tail flicking behind him.

"No, wait," I called, taking another step. "I'm not here to hurt you. I'm trying to help. Nox found me and my friend in the forest, we're trying to get to the Quartz Tower..."

"She is a Dorothy," the Fox man growled. "What were you thinking?"

"No, no, I'm not. I mean, I kind of am—" I responded quickly, trying to reassure him, but I was clearly making it worse. I took a deep breath. "I'm not here to hurt anyone. Please..."

With my attention firmly on the fox, I was hardly aware of movement to my right. I glanced over and noticed Nox had shifted back to his human form, holding the small fox tightly in the crook of his arm, scrabbling to get free.

With his free hand, he smoothed the fur on the cub's back and set it on the ground. "Hear her out, Bartlett."

Another fox crept from the mound, this one slighter in build and wearing a plain blue dress. She, too, rose onto her hind legs and sniffed the air.

"Sosha," Nox greeted, nodding his head.

She looked directly at me, her ears erect and twitching, then turned and scurried back below ground.

I sighed. "Nox, this is a bad idea. I appreciate the gesture, but I don't want these people to be afraid in their own home. I'll head back, find Fallon, and move as far east as I can tomorrow. Hopefully, we can find another way to the fortress when we're done."

I turned toward the trees when a small voice said, "Wait."

I glanced back to see the cub running toward me and turned, crouching to be closer to its level and hopefully less of a threat.

He was cute, apparently not afraid of me at all, but that wasn't surprising given he'd just been chewing on a lion.

"Are you a Dorothy?" he asked, his little tail swishing behind him.

I swallowed and looked to Nox. He remained still, giving me no indication of how to proceed.

"Dorothy was my great grandma," I answered, "and the stories about her aren't exactly true. She was blamed for things that weren't her fault and I've come here to help put things right."

"Momma!" the little guy exclaimed, his tail wagging excitedly. "Momma, she isn't a Dorothy."

The female reemerged, standing behind her partner, and looking at me.

"Let her explain," Nox suggested. "She won't hurt you. She helped me out when she could easily have harmed me," he informed them, indicating the healing wound on his shoulder. "Just hear what she has to say and I'll escort her back. You can draw your own conclusions."

The cub raced back to his parents and as they sat beside the fire, I saw Nox pat the ground beside him.

I rose and walked slowly toward them, sitting a couple of feet away from him.

"Did you land in a house too?" the little guy questioned, gazing at me from between his parents.

I smiled. "No, I was brought here by someone Glinda sent to find me."

The two larger foxes flinched at the mention of Glinda, so I quickly added, "But I don't serve her, I'm friends with lots of people in the West."

Nox raised a hand. "Please."

I looked to him for reassurance and he smiled, then nodded and encouraged, "Go ahead. Tell them everything you told me."

* * *

WALKING BACK THROUGH THE FOREST, I waited until the den was well behind us before I asked, "Why did you do that?"

Nox shrugged. "I figured people need to make up their own minds before the story is twisted. If you really are who you say you are, you're going to need some support. Best to lay the foundations now."

"So you believe me?"

He nodded his head once. "Things have to change. The way I see it, people can't keep living like this. We have to make a choice sometime, and I figure choosing to live in peace, freely, is a good way to go."

I was about to thank him when an arrow whistled past my ear.

"She's fine, Fallon," Nox called in an exasperated voice. "But you knew that since she's walking back to your camp."

He stepped out from behind a tree and stalked toward me, slinging his bow over his shoulder.

When he reached me, he took my face in both hands and pressed his forehead against mine.

"I'm fine, really. I'm sorry we left you, but Nox had something, someone, he wanted me to see. They were scared. If we all went they'd have hidden."

He pulled back, frowning in confusion.

"A family of foxes," I explained. "Fox people. They've lived here in hiding for years. They have kids. There are hundreds of families all waiting for a safer time. All waiting for something to happen that makes their lives better. Nox thought—"

"That if she got her side of the story over first, then they'd be more likely to rally behind her than hide here and hear whatever Wyrm shit Glinda spreads."

Fallon scowled. I wasn't sure if it was at the mention of Glinda or that Nox was talking to him. Or even that he'd finished my sentence for me. I wasn't certain what had caused his reaction, but I was more concerned with calming Fallon than picking another fight with Nox.

"I'm sorry," I murmured quietly, kissing his cheek.

He kissed me back, then turned and walked into the forest.

I looked at Nox, annoyed with his interference, and mouthed, "What the hell was that?"

Missing my point, he shrugged and followed, leaving me to trail behind.

CHAPTER 7

We returned to our little camp and managed to grab a few hours of sleep.

The mist was clearing when I woke up, and Fallon was still in a deep sleep. With little idea what time it was, since I couldn't see the sun for trees, I lay still for a few moments.

Fallon had his arm wrapped tightly around my waist, I assumed to keep me from disappearing into the forest without him again, so I remained where I was and closed my eyes.

Then I remembered Nox.

I sat bolt upright, making Fallon follow and reach for the nearest weapon.

"Where's Nox?" I inquired, looking around. "He was by the fire when I went to sleep."

The fire was still burning, suggesting it had been topped up with wood recently, but there was no sign of him in either of his forms.

I turned to Fallon, who gave me a look that said what did you expect?

Honestly, I hadn't expected anything—I was still just

grateful he hadn't killed me—but after the previous night, I thought he'd stick around to at least say goodbye.

Not sharing my concern, Fallon began to unpack breakfast.

"Let me," I volunteered, reaching for the bag.

He gave a stern shake of his head and continued, handing me a flask of water and small bread roll. He didn't look directly at me, making his mood clear.

"You're still angry with me."

He glanced up.

"I had to trust him, Fallon. Okay, I should have woken you but—"

I stopped talking as he looked up, his eyes blazing with fury clear in their depths.

"I said I was sorry."

He cocked his head and raised his brows.

"It should make it okay. Yeah."

He looked away.

"Really. You have to trust me sometime. You can't always be there to save me. Maybe I shouldn't have trusted him, but he did give me the opportunity to tell my side of this crappy story to some of the people most horribly affected by my family's involvement here. This is probably going to get a hell of a lot worse before it gets better, and if I can avoid being held entirely responsible for it, maybe even gather some allies, I'm going to do it."

He closed his eyes and sighed, his shoulders sagging. I hated seeing him battling with his emotions with no way to talk them through.

"Fallon... I don't want to fight. I understand you're angry but—"

He held up a hand.

"Not angry?"

He shook his head and gave me a small, rueful smile.

"Just disappointed," I corrected.

He nodded.

"You know that's worse, right?"

He shrugged, pointed at me, then made a fist, before opening his hand quickly and splaying his fingers.

"I know. But I hadn't gone far."

He threw up his hands in exasperation.

"Okay, no, you didn't know that, and I've said I'm sorry, can't we just..." My voice shook. I'd never seen him so passionate in an exchange. I felt bad I'd made him so angry, but he had to understand I was able to make my own decisions.

He stopped what he was doing and walked my way. When he reached me, he pulled me to my feet and held me close, cradling my head against his chest, and I could hear his heart beating, the fear that something had happened to me etched in each rapid thump.

"I didn't know it was going to take so long," I admitted, as he kissed my head and stroked my hair. We stood there are a few minutes, him holding me, and me trying to find the words I needed to properly apologize without sounding like I was just making excuses. Eventually, I suggested, "We should get going."

He stepped back and nodded, then resumed packing the bag. I rolled our blankets and kicked loose earth over the fire before looking around the spot where we'd stayed.

"I think that's everything," I muttered, as he shouldered the pack. "Are you ready?"

He nodded and ran his hand over my back, allowing me to go first.

"You know, sitting here last night, Nox mentioned Sayer.

Well, I mentioned Sayer, but Nox said he was a traitor. Does everyone believe that?"

I glanced back and watched as he nodded.

"Is he?" I asked. "I mean, I know I should trust him. I've no reason to doubt him, and I also know he's been walking the line, but could he have... could he be a threat?"

He caught me by the hand and turned me to face him, pressing his lips together into a grim line.

"I know... it's just we haven't heard a thing for, how long has it been? I can't keep track. What if she does get to him?"

He stroked my cheek and shook his head slowly.

"You're certain?"

He nodded once.

"Can we trust Nox?" I inquired, locking eyes with him. I wanted his raw opinion.

He held out a hand and tilted it left then right.

"So-so? But last night was a good sign, right? I mean, he introduced me to people who've been hiding for years. Then he brought me back to you. I know he took off this morning, but that doesn't have to mean he's up to something sinister, does it?"

He took a deep breath and I could tell the shake of his head was reluctant.

"So, we trust him?"

He sighed and nodded, and I turned around and started walking again. "Okay, I feel a bit better now... when do you think we'll see Sayer next? Is Glinda going to send him when we reach the tower? Will she come herself? Do you really think she'll attack me, or do you think she'll try to find a way around it?"

He tapped me on the shoulder, and I stopped my nervous rambling.

He stepped around me and pointed at my chest. I looked

down at his hand, and he splayed his fingers then used his thumb to signal over his shoulder.

I smiled. "Okay, let's get there first."

His smile was reassuring as he reached for me and pulled me into his chest. We stayed there for a few moments together. Just us. He kissed the top of my head and ran his hand softly up and down my back, comforting me and teasing the nervous tension away.

When he pulled back and looked down at me, he seemed pleased I'd finally shut up.

"Thank you," I murmured as he placed a gentle kiss on my lips.

He nodded once, smiled, and turned around, taking the lead.

I followed without question. I was happy to follow Fallon.

* * *

We stopped for lunch the same as the day before. The trees in this part of the forest were heavily grown over with moss, which made finding somewhere to sit a challenge. Every time I chose a place to sit and got comfortable, moisture seeped through, making me yelp in discomfort. With aching feet I really needed to rest up, if only for a few minutes. I was tired. I was uncomfortable. I was furious with Glinda for oh so many things, and annoyed with Sayer for not finding a way to tell me everything I needed to know. Nox had really ground my gears, causing so much tension with Fallon before taking off and leaving us to it. Asshole.

In the end, I gave up and just changed my pants. The shoes were amazingly helpful for that.

We were about to continue on when I heard twigs snapping.

"Decided to come back, did you?" I teased as a tuft of black fur came into view. I looked for his eyes, but I didn't find a pair of warm amber orbs—it wasn't a lion.

Fallon moved with lightning speed, positioning himself between me and the oversized wolf.

I didn't tell him not to hurt it. Not this time. There was something about its body language that told me it wasn't going to negotiate.

Fallon swung his sword and the wolf backed up, snarling. The sound echoed behind me, and I spun to see three more equally vicious wolves closing in.

When Nox had approached, there had been something about him, I didn't quite know what, that told me not to harm him. That he wasn't a threat. Perhaps I could sense the humanity in him, maybe the difference was in his eyes, since his were a warm amber and these beasts had eyes of piercing light blue. Whatever it was, I had no such feeling now.

"Fallon, I know I said don't kill stuff, but..." I trailed off, leaving the rest unsaid as the one facing Fallon snarled again and I turned sharply, raising a hand.

On command, a blast of icy wind swept through the trees, causing the boughs to creak and crack. The wolf in front of us crouched, baring its teeth, and I turned to check the other three.

They'd done the same and were creeping forward. It was almost as though they knew how to counter the wind.

Fallon broke away from me, leaving me behind with the three wolves. I didn't know if he was aware of them or not, but he was busy dealing with the leader of their small pack.

"Shit..." I groaned, realizing I had nothing to defend

myself with but Fallon's small dagger. We were stuck, there was nowhere to run, and no time to try and climb to safety.

Thinking through whatever options we had, I remembered how easily I'd hovered over the battlefield the day Tatiana's Lioneag fought with the monkeys.

"Fallon," I called, reaching for him. He didn't hear me, too focused on the wolf stalking toward him, so I grasped the collar of his shirt and sprang upward.

The wind took us, sweeping us up into the boughs of the closest tree. The wolves leapt forward, snarling and snapping their jaws as they jumped up at the fat trunk. I found my footing on a branch and released Fallon's collar, turning and grabbing the tree trunk. My hands slipped several times on the wet moss coating the bark, and I was beginning to panic. If I fell, I wasn't sure I could defend myself. If Fallon fell, I wasn't sure I could defend him.

Fallon gained his balance almost immediately and pushed me into the trunk while I gained my footing, then he reached instinctively for his most trusted weapon, but his bow was gone. He turned to me with a look of confusion on his face, when a sudden roar drew the wolves' attention.

I couldn't make out the direction it had come from, but the wolves seemed to know, as they all turned away from our refuge and formed a semicircle facing north.

Another roar.

This was quieter but came from the south, and the wolves repositioned. I reached for Fallon and tapped his shoulder.

"Where's your bow?"

He scanned the ground and pointed.

"Shit." There was no way he could get down there without the wolves spotting him. "Is that Nox?"

He looked back at me with an expression I took to mean, 'I hope so.'

"What do we do? Wait here and see, or make a run for it?"

He held up his hand and scanned the ground again. I looked down to see the wolves had closed ranks, still facing south. There was no more sound from the forest.

"Is there more than one?" I questioned quietly, watching the wolves' ears twitch. One of them turned and faced north, the other three crouching and snarling at something to the south. Their hackles were raised, tails hung low, as they waited and we watched.

Twigs snapped below a few meters to my right and I turned my head, hoping to catch a glimpse of whatever was stalking in the dense forest. I couldn't see anything and glanced back to Fallon, to see he'd moved from the branch beside mine to one lower down. He was facing my way, watching the pack at the foot of the tree.

"Hey," I called in a loud whisper.

He scowled up at me and pointed to where his bow lay.

I shook my head, but he wasn't looking. His attention was firmly fixed on the wolf facing north.

Was that the leader? They all looked the same to me and I'd lost track of which was which.

Before I could think any more on it, there was a low growl from one of the trio facing south and out of nowhere, Nox pounced.

Despite his size he was fast, capturing the wolf's neck in his jaws and dragging it to the ground effortlessly. I could see the force he used to crush the animal's windpipe, and it kicked and struggled uselessly under his weight.

It was a brutal death, but rather him than me.

The other three reacted a second later, and so did Fallon.

He hung from the branch he was standing on, hanging there for a moment before dropping to the ground. He landed perfectly, bending his knees to absorb the impact and rolling off to the side to retrieve his bow.

By the time the three wolves had caught up with Nox, Fallon had an arrow nocked.

How he took aim and fired so quickly, while the three wolves were moving around so much, fighting to lock their jaws on any part of the lion's body, was anyone's guess.

His arrow pierced the side of the wolf nearest and it yelped, before falling to the ground.

With one less enemy pinning him down, Nox was able to roll over, pulling the wolf still caught in his jaws with him.

The wolves on his back released him, only to spring toward his exposed underside. But one misjudged, tearing into his trapped companion instead, and Nox took the chance to regain his footing as another arrow struck one of the remaining wolves in the eye.

It yowled in pain, spinning and rolling, trying to dislodge it, but it was deeply embedded, and the creature was clearly becoming weakened.

Another twang of the bowstring as Fallon fired. This one missed its mark, but pulled the two remaining wolves' attention to him.

I turned my head, looking where he'd last been, but he had moved to get out of view of the remaining wolves. If they took off after him, Nox would have to give chase and that would put him at a disadvantage.

With just two wolves left to fight off, Nox appeared to have the advantage, and I concentrated on getting myself down from the tree.

In the end, I jumped. My landing wasn't graceful but it did the job, and I rushed to Fallon.

"Are you okay?"

He nodded and approached one of the wolves, pulling the arrow he'd used to kill it from its body.

"I'm fine," Nox muttered, kicking one of them in the head, "thanks for asking."

I turned around and checked him over for injuries. His hair was a mess, and there were a few scratches on his arms and legs. "Sorry. Thank you. We thought you'd left us."

He tipped back his head, shaking his braids. "I had. Then I heard the pack had been seen around the city ruins and came to check on you. Good thing I did, otherwise you'd have been stuck up that tree all night."

I looked down awkwardly. I'd been so angry with him before, and then he'd risked his life to help us with those monstrous things. "That was good of you, thank you."

He crouched to examine the dead wolf he'd just kicked, checking its coat and mouth. "These are unusually large. I'm inclined to think they belong to your friendly southern friend. Their pelts will come in handy for someone, and their meat will feed the birds, so they won't be wasted out here. Can you wait an hour so I can let the people know they're here to be skinned, and I'll escort you the rest of the way?"

I looked sideways to Fallon, seeking his opinion. When he nodded his agreement, I turned back to Nox and replied, "We appreciate it. Thanks."

Without another word he turned and walked into the forest, and I moved back to the tree I'd hidden in.

"Suppose I should get comfortable," I muttered, sitting on a large, exposed root, looking at the four corpses scattered around. "Why do you suppose he's changed his mind about us?"

Fallon looked in the direction Nox had disappeared in and narrowed his eyes.

"You still don't fully trust him?" I asked.

He shrugged.

I understood how he felt. It was hard to know who was a friend, but I couldn't suspect everyone of being an enemy. If I did that, I'd never have gotten to the fortress and I wouldn't have Fallon.

We certainly wouldn't have Sayer.

I still trusted him. I had no reason not to, regardless of what Nox had said. He hadn't done anything to harm me. He'd kept me safe. He'd helped me and continued to lie to Glinda about us.

But that could just be more lies. More deceit. Him saving his own skin.

No. I couldn't let thoughts like that in. I'd come too far. I wouldn't turn against him. I needed him as much as I needed Fallon and our new ally.

CHAPTER 8

*N*ox returned wearing different shorts and a heavy belt. As soon as he arrived, we set off walking and continued to do so until long after nightfall. I was waiting for Fallon to indicate he was ready to stop. He, it seemed, was waiting for Nox or me to indicate it was too dark to continue.

"So, you have no idea what you're capable of?" Nox asked.

I'd been waiting for him to bring that up, so I shrugged, and started, "No. I mean, when Tatiana's Lioneag and the flying monkey—"

"You're walking into enemy territory with a mute archer and hitherto untested magical abilities," he interrupted, pointing out the obvious.

"Well, yeah, but—"

"You need to work out what you can do before you get to the tower. The people living in the area aren't likely to want to harm you, but you can be sure there's someone or something waiting to intercept you. Glinda will have this meticulously planned."

"But Sayer—"

"Can't be trusted," he replied crisply.

I stopped walking and turned to Fallon, but he looked away. I wasn't sure what that meant and looked for somewhere to sit, both mentally and physically weary. The two of them may have been prepared to walk into the night, but my feet were killing me, and I was getting hungry. "What makes you think that?" I demanded. His cryptic shade throwing was pissing me off.

Nox looked around us and began to gather twigs. A glance at Fallon told me he was gathering larger sticks and fallen branches for a fire. Building a small mound between us, Nox took what looked like flint and tinder from a pouch at his belt and began striking, then answered, "His people were locked in a building and burned. Who started that fire, Fallon?"

I shook my head and looked between them. "No... he wouldn't—"

Fallon lowered his head.

Closing my eyes briefly, I took a deep, steadying breath. I didn't care what they said, I wasn't prepared to believe he was capable of that.

"Okay... all that aside, I agree. I do need to get some magic practice in," I blurted, ready to change the subject. "I just haven't had time or anywhere safe to do it. I left the fortress after a few days of taking over, and I don't even know how many days it has been now... how long have I even been here?"

"I believe about two weeks, from the information I have," Nox said.

I glared at him. "And what information is that?"

"I hear all kinds of things from all kinds of people," he said, shrugging. "Glinda can't stop the birds from singing."

I looked to Fallon who nodded his agreement.

"Two weeks? Is that all? Feels like so much longer... how far is it to... where are we headed?"

"The western villages. Glinda calls it Munchkinland, which is nothing short of insulting. It was her sister's doing. She mocked the people for their short stature, naming them Munchkins and treating them like children. They never once complained, but my people hated the witches for it. I still hate them for it."

I nodded. I knew what he meant. My great grandma had described the people of the west in much the same way as it seemed Glinda had addressed them. Even though it was over a hundred years ago and I tried to tell myself people were less respectful of anyone with differences—my great grandmother's mental state making her one such person—it irked me. I tried not to focus on it too much and questioned, "How far away are we?"

"From here? A half a day's walk to the town. The Quartz Tower is half a day's walk northeast of there, plus the climb, so it's probably best we spend the night in town and set out first thing. The largest of the villages is likely to have buildings we'd be more comfortable in."

He seemed to know a lot about these places, more than I would have expected, but I let it go. I'd find out soon enough and I didn't want to start second guessing his honesty. I'd been complaining enough about the lack of trust going around, it would be hypocritical to start doing so myself. "So, we should stop here?" I asked, looking around.

The place didn't look like a suitable place to light a fire. The trees were sparse, not as old as the ones deeper in the forest, and these had a few sick-looking leaves clinging to their branches. The ground was muddy, not good to sleep on, so I turned to Fallon and said, "I'm going to create something for us to sleep in, okay?"

He glanced to Nox for his reaction, then nodded.

Nox cocked his head.

"What?" I queried, looking at an open space beside him.

"You can propel yourself on a breeze and build shelters well enough, but that isn't going to be enough to protect your people, you know?"

I narrowed my eyes, trying to ignore him as our accommodation for the night materialized. I was aware of my shortcomings. Painfully aware. But it wasn't as though the new abilities I'd gained came with a manual.

"You say you want to help," he continued, "but so far you haven't really done much, have you?"

I didn't like his tone one bit. He was talking to me as though I'd volunteered for this. Sure, I'd agreed to help, but I didn't receive a formal invitation or anything.

"Where are you going with this?" I snapped, walking toward the little wooden house I'd made. Fallon did the same and we left Nox standing in the muddy clearing.

"Just stating facts, Ella. You can't win a war without training. If the people could have won it without your help, they'd have done it by now, don't you think?"

I pushed open the door and stepped inside. There was a stove on the right hand wall, and three beds lined up opposite. Along the rear wall was a table stacked with necessary utensils, with three chairs pushed in around it.

"Right. So what do you want me to do?" I called, as Fallon kicked off his boots and lay on the bed closest to the door.

I glanced back and saw Nox had followed us into the house. He was leaning against the doorframe, staring at me. "I think you need to find out what you're capable of."

I laughed as I sorted through the utensils on the table. "You're going to teach me magic, are you? What do you know about it?"

I put the iron pan on the stove.

Hearing movement behind me, I turned to come face to chest with him. I tried to step back but the table was in the way so was forced to lift my head.

His amber eyes were narrowed and his jaw was set. "I knew a sorceress once. We trained together. She provided me shots to dodge, I provided her a target. I considered offering you the same."

"You'd help me?" I asked skeptically.

Fallon snorted and I shot him a look. I hadn't meant to sound so incredulous.

Nox folded his arms across his chest. "I'm already helping you."

Fallon's mouth turned down in the corners and he shrugged.

"Well, yeah," I stumbled, feeling a bit like I'd been called out for being a brat. "I just didn't expect you to want to help me like that."

Nox took a deep breath and sighed. "It's really in everyone's interests that I do."

I frowned. "So, you believe me?"

He smirked. "I suppose I must. Get yourself something to eat and we'll have a try out."

I glanced back at Fallon. He'd picked up the pack and was looking through whatever food we had left. I didn't know why, it would be the same cured meats, cheeses, and bread. After two days of eating that stuff, I was missing Orla's gourd soups, as macabre as they were. I was starving. "Okay," I agreed, holding out a hand for Fallon to pass me the ham from the pack. "But don't complain if I hurt you."

Nox laughed as I inched away. "Just don't singe the mane."

I frowned. "Fire?"

"If my assumptions are correct, you control air and fire elements. Tatiana possesses earth, not that she uses it at all, since she prefers her sword. That leaves—"

"Water," I finished, interrupting him. "That explains her going everywhere in bubbles."

Nox laughed again. "Don't underestimate her bubbles. They're her shields and are damn hard to pop."

"But they can be? Popped, I mean."

"Needs to be something very sharp, or I expect heat would damage them, but yes."

I cut three generous slices from the ham and placed one on each plate, then turned to look at Fallon. He'd left the pack on the bed closest me and lay back down. He seemed comfortable enough, and not at all concerned about the conversation I was having with Nox.

Without a word I continued to serve dinner, thinking about the issue of Glinda having shields. I didn't know enough about them to have a plan in place. It seemed I was working on the fly there.

Finally, I took a skin of ale from the pack and poured three cups before packing the bag and sitting down. "Okay, let's eat and get the training over with."

Fallon seemed distant as we ate, and I wanted to ask him about it but wasn't sure how to raise the subject with Nox in the room. So, we ate in silence and when we were done, I asked, "Do you want to get ready and I'll come out when I've cleared this away?"

Without answering, Nox took my plate and Fallon's, and placed them on the table. "Leave them. Are you coming out, Fallon?"

He lay back on the bed and put his hands behind his head. Apparently not.

"Fair enough. Ready, witchy?"

I scowled and walked toward the door. "Do not make that my pet name," I warned, already feeling nervous and irritable.

Nox laughed behind me and I looked down at Fallon. "We won't be long. I'll stay in view of the house."

Fallon smiled but didn't bother to open his eyes. I shook my head and stepped out into the woods. He'd gone from being entirely untrusting of Nox, to relaxed enough to just doze while Nox helped me work on my magic.

A few meters from the house, I stopped walking. My boots were sinking into the mud, and I hoped I wouldn't have to move too much.

"So, you've got big gusts of wind covered, and the general use of magic for day to day necessities," Nox noted from behind me.

"Yep," I replied, not turning around. "But I think that's the shoes."

"Witch of the East shoes?"

I nodded. "They attached to my feet the second Sayer began moving me here. And they were silver. They were silver for Great Grandma Dorothy, too, she only used them to get home, but apparently they let me do what I want, more or less. And they change. Like, when I arrived at Glinda's place they were more something I'd wear... well, they weren't appropriate. Now they conform to my needs, they're red, and... they just change."

He was quiet for a moment, then inquired, "What did you do when Tatiana attacked?"

I thought back to that awful day and looked down at my

hands. "I stopped time. Or at least, that's what I tried to do. Whatever it was, the whole scene was frozen."

"You didn't attack?"

I shook my head. "I'm not really a fan of violence. I'd rather sort things out diplomatically."

"So you stopped the battle and talked it out?"

I shrugged. "The monkeys, they were being slaughtered. I made sure Tatiana knew how I felt about her stunt, so the air's been cleared, but it wasn't until a while after when we really talked everything through."

He was standing right behind me. I didn't need him to touch me for me to be aware of his presence. He was large and imposing enough.

"This can't be done diplomatically," he informed me, his voice a deep hum in my ear. "You have to fight. You'll have to defend your people using whatever force is necessary. People will die on both sides, and you're going to be partially responsible for that, but the alternative is to hand Ozacia over to Glinda and allow her to rule as she sees fit."

"How will she rule?" I asked quietly.

Nox stepped around me and lifted my chin with a finger. His amber eyes searched mine, and I turned my head away. There was an intimacy in his actions that I wasn't ready for. Not with him. Sayer and Fallon were more than enough, weren't they? "You really want to know?"

I nodded.

"Totally. Cruelly."

"What proof do you have of that?" I countered. The more I learned of Glinda, the more it seemed she'd manipulated, well, everyone. My great grandma, the people of Oz. She'd planned murders to take Oz over and the one person who could challenge her didn't have the confidence. At least with Tati alive, the people had someone to rally behind.

He stepped back from me but didn't lower his gaze. He held me there, forcing me to give him my attention.

I shifted from one foot to the other, waiting. There was something in the intensity of his amber eyes that made my stomach squirm. I swallowed. I didn't want to feel that, not now. Not with him. But I couldn't look away. A couple of seconds ticked by and he looked down at the ground and explained, "When her attack came, it was swift. She swept down on the city with no notice, setting the outlying residences ablaze. The people panicked and ran to the center, seeking aid from the wizard.

"Of course he wasn't as powerful as he was purported, and when her army closed in, the palace was packed with helpless lambs and few able to protect them.

"My people, black and yellow alike, were the only defenders they had, and defend them we did.

"We were brutal. But she even more brutal. We were fierce, but her numbers were great. Her Horners were front line, boiling us in our skins if their lightning bolts made contact. Her Hoppers crushed the skulls of the little folk. And her soldiers... many of my people were traumatized by what they were forced to do to her*them*.

"We were outnumbered a hundred to one, and it wasn't long before she overpowered us. She made us watch as she drowned the wizard in a pretty bubble of water. His loyal and loving people watched him writhe on the ground as his body fought for breath, powerless to help him. Children wailed, men and women alike wept for him, but they couldn't stand up to her. None of us could save that man.

"She took up residence in the palace and waited for her sister, but Tatiana didn't come. We were separated. We were brought before her to swear fealty. The weakest did. The strongest stood silent before her and were tortured for our insolence.

"When Tatiana finally arrived, the people were broken. They were mourning. They were afraid. They fled the moment the sisters began to fight.

"The seismic force of Tatiana's power brought the city down. A number of us remained, initially to allow the escapees to gain a head start, but in the end, we were simply watching and waiting for the victor to decide our fate.

"The fight raged for hours with no clear result. Evenly matched, there couldn't be a winner. It was Tatiana who called for a pause.

"She proposed the truce, promising never to stray over the southern border, provided Glinda kept out of the North and ceased her attacks. Glinda demanded control of the East. Tatiana agreed, stipulating she gained guardianship of the West.

"Then came mention of stewards. Tatiana had never claimed one, declaring the practice outdated and unnecessary. Glinda's steward had fallen in the first wave of attacks, and she called for all those born to a steward to step forward.

"Fallon came first. He was bloodied and exhausted, without a single arrow left in his quiver, his sword notched and bent, but he wasn't beaten. When Glinda approached he spat at her feet. When she struck him he looked straight into her eyes and told her he would rather burn than spend a day in her service.

"With that silky smile she has, she extended a single finger and prodded him in the throat, she said, 'You will never speak to me with such disrespect again.' We all watched in horror as he began to choke, blood spurting from his mouth. Fallon fell to his knees, clawing at his throat, and Bree broke from the gathered stewards and rushed to attend him.

"Glinda was pleased with her response and told her to leave him and come to her. But another stepped forward and said, 'Lady Glinda, good Witch of the South, most beautiful of the rulers of Ozaci, all my life I have trained to serve but never believed the opportunity to serve you would ever present itself. I beg of you not to choose her. Take me, I will better meet your needs than she ever could.'

"Glinda has always fallen for flattery, but flattery from a pretty boy with golden hair and a dashing smile was sure to win her over, and so she took her steward and returned to her lands, her forces turning and marching south the instant she was gone.

"Tatiana remained, assisting Bree in treating Fallon and then the other wounded, and eventually we went our separate ways. Fallon returned to the East, I followed my people into the forests, Tatiana returned to her lands with Bree, and Glinda planned her next move," Nox finished, as I stared at him with wide eyes.

"Which was?" I prompted, even though I didn't really want to know. I was already close to tears from hearing his recount of her despicable treatment of the people of this world, but I had to know.

"She came for us, and won," he replied simply. "So, you see, Ella, without you we're doomed. Tatiana can't stop her. The people can't stop her. You're the last hope this world has for being free. It's a lot, I appreciate that, but many weaker than you have made greater sacrifices. Your great grandmother, for instance. Her innocence was taken from her. A young girl shouldn't witness what she did. It was cruel. But the people of Oz have lost far more. They've witnessed far worse. We can't survive her destruction much longer."

"What if I'm not enough?" I questioned, suddenly unsure of our quest after hearing the amount of power Glinda had.

His expression changed and his eyes softened as he looked at me, with a small smile tugging the corner of his mouth. "You're more than enough," he murmured, and the expression on his face told me he believed his words.

I looked away, brushing my hair back from my face and changed the subject. "So, you think I can make fire?"

He smirked, aware of what I just did. "I know you can do far more than just make fire. Hit me."

* * *

FALLON WAS STILL on the bed where we'd left him when we returned. He did manage to push himself up on his elbows and give me a questioning look when I collapsed on my own cot in the center of the room.

"I can do fire," I announced, staring at the ceiling. I was exhausted.

Nox laughed and edged around the room to the cot behind mine. "She's a natural, now that she knows what she's feeling for."

Natural was stretching things a bit, but I had managed to create fire and I was very happy with myself. What surprised me was how much Nox seemed to know about the process, especially since he had no magical ability himself—shifting excluded.

"Yeah," I agreed, taking a deep breath. "It's about feeling for it. Thank you."

His cot creaked as he lay down. "Happy to help."

I turned over to face Fallon. He was still leaning up on his elbows looking down at me, and raised his brows once.

I could tell he was asking me if I was okay.

I smiled. He seemed much less concerned about me spending time with Nox now. It appeared our little practice session was enough to set Fallon's mind at ease. I was glad. I clearly needed both of them to help me get this done, and they needed me if they wanted a chance at freeing Oz from Glinda.

He nodded once then lay down, and I curled up tighter where I lay, relieved to have some kind of harmony between us. We needed it if we were going to succeed.

We had to succeed.

$\mathcal{N}$ine

"ARE YOU JUST LEAVING IT THERE?" Nox asked the next morning, as I closed the front door of the small house we'd slept in.

I'd slept surprisingly well after spending several hours out in the forest with Nox.

"Yep," I said, taking Fallon's offered hand. "Might need it on the way back."

Nox nodded. "I assumed you didn't know how to take it down."

Fallon snorted and I jabbed him in the ribs with my elbow.

Learning what had happened to the city and how Fallon had lost his voice explained a few things. Like why he reacted the way he did to Glinda touching him, and why he remained loyal to Sayer despite the things he'd done. It made me feel a little better knowing exactly how he'd ended up in her service.

It also made me more determined to take the West.

I hated violence. I could handle myself well enough, I had to given the attention I got working in a strip club, but I didn't like using force. It was the same as carrying the small pistol in my purse, I did it because I had to protect myself, but didn't want to use it. I pulled it on Sayer, admittedly, but I didn't intend to shoot him.

I'd make an exception for Glinda.

"And that," I admitted with a nod of my head, "but if there are people living in the forest who could use a comfortable bed, even for just one night, it doesn't hurt to leave it up, does it?"

Nox shrugged noncommittally and kept moving.

As we moved farther east the trees changed dramatically. The few sparse leaves I'd noticed back when we'd stopped for the night had become a heavy canopy above our heads. The muddy ground had evened out and was covered with a thick carpet of grass. Flowers had begun to spring up, and birds could be heard singing high above.

It wasn't long before we joined the yellow brick road. Unlike the state it had been in while we were in the South, here it was carefully tended, each brick clean and bright in the morning sun breaking through the canopy of the trees.

"Is there anything I need to know before we reach this place?" I inquired, as we walked over an ornate little bridge to cross a bubbling stream. "Like, don't tell them who I am because they'll cut off my head without bothering to listen to why I'm here, or don't make eye contact with the men or the women will eat me alive?" I teased, trying to lighten the growing tension building inside me.

"The mayor will have questions, but he won't turn you away," Nox replied with a roll of his eyes.

I gave him a skeptical look.

"Really," he promised, looking at Fallon for backup. "They're good people. Fair."

Fallon nodded once and I smiled at him. He gave me a rueful grin in return and I frowned.

"What happened here?" I asked Fallon in a whisper, trusting him to tell me the truth. "How badly has she treated them?"

Fallon raised his right hand moved it in front of his body.

"Later?"

He nodded. That would be an interesting conversation.

I turned and took in our surroundings—the town seemed deserted.

"They'll have seen us coming. I expect we'll be—" Nox was cut off when someone called his name.

"Nox!"

I looked around for some indication of where the voice had come from. It sounded like a child, but I didn't want to assume so kept my mouth shut.

My suspicion was confirmed when I heard rapping on the window of a nearby cottage. As I turned to face the building, I saw the curtains at the window pull tightly shut, so I looked away.

"I think we should just pass through," I muttered, already feeling unwelcome.

Fallon shook his head and took my hand.

"They're just being cautious," Nox said, walking on.

We followed in silence, walking through the narrow, abandoned streets with our heads down.

It wasn't until we emerged in a town square when Nox stopped and turned to face me.

"I'll give the mayor a heads up, although I'm sure he already knows we're here," Nox offered, his voice casual.

Just then, a door on my right swung open and five men dressed in chain mail, holding pikes, rushed out.

Each of the guards were around four feet tall, their gait clumsy as they maneuvered the long weapons, which were as awkward for them as their heavy, protective clothing.

They formed an arc around the door, and I looked past them to the figure emerging behind. He was around the same height but clearly older, and the bearded gentleman was dressed in a dark green suit with a white shirt and matching green cravat. His salt and pepper beard was neatly groomed, and gave him a friendly appearance.

"Miss Rose," he began, stepping out. "Welcome to Middletown. We expected you days ago."

I was surprised by his friendly greeting. "You did?"

He nodded, stepping between two of his guards. They all lowered their weapons and seemed to visibly relax.

"So," the mayor said, looking at the three of us, "you found her, Nox."

I glanced his way to see him grin.

"I said I would. Has she been back?" I assumed he was speaking about Glinda, but I remained quiet as I watched their interaction.

The mayor shook his head. "No. She'll send the sorcerer, no doubt. Are the other rumors true?"

Nox looked from me to Fallon and laughed. "And then some."

"What's that supposed to mean?" I demanded, turning to face him, and irritated with his cocky comment. "I wasn't aware you were gathering information about me. What have you come up with?"

Nox looked at me, his lips twitching up in the corners. "You're emotionally involved with the stewards of the West and South."

My defenses immediately went up. I didn't like being judged for the people I cared about, especially by someone I'd just met. His eyes fixed on the line forming between my brows as I snapped, "That's nobody's business. And Fallon is *not* a steward."

Nox smirked and turned back to the mayor, then continued, "So the sorcerer's allegiance is still unclear. It seems Tatiana believes him to be hers, while her sister believes the opposite. Then there's Ellana."

"What about me?" I interjected, getting frustrated as he kept me out of a conversation about me, like I wasn't here. This was my quest, after all, and I was the one trying to help people. I was tired of people being cryptic, especially when they were supposed to be aiding me.

"Whose is he?" Nox pressed, turning to me. There was a challenge in his voice that I didn't like, and I blinked at him as I tried to figure out what he was asking. "Sayer, is he yours?"

"What do you mean, 'whose?' He doesn't belong to anyone," I stated firmly.

His eyes slid to Fallon.

"And him," I snapped. "I don't know what messed up rules you've been living by here, but where I come from people don't own people. Looks like it's something you all need to adopt."

"Miss Rose," the mayor interrupted, holding up a hand. "No offence was meant. Please, come inside and allow me to explain some things. Perhaps with a clearer picture of what is afoot here, you will be better equipped to complete the task set before you."

He turned and went back through the door he'd come out of, his band of guards falling either side of the entrance.

I looked up at the building before I followed. It was a single story with a thatched roof, running a good distance along the path through the village. Assuming it was the town hall, I looked over my shoulder to Fallon and tilted my head, requesting he come too.

The mayor pushed open the wooden internal door, explaining, "I spend much of my time here but live in the cottage opposite." He waved his hand by his head to indicate it was behind him. "This is where we keep the annals. All visits are well documented, and I took a special interest in your great grandmother's visit when I took office here."

With Fallon following, I stepped inside and trailed the mayor through the entrance vestibule.

"I'm sure you know the details. Her house landed on the then ruler of these lands, killing her instantly. As a result, the magical footwear she wore transferred to your great grandmother. Since she was the one who conquered the witch, she acquired the power locked in the tower and also took ownership of her magical slippers." He'd walked into a long hall and paused, turning around to look pointedly down at my feet—at my glinting, red converse sneakers. "Garnets?" he added, surprised.

I smiled uncertainly. "Yeah. Not sure why they ended up like this," I admitted. "They just appeared on my feet when Sayer—"

I stopped talking. I didn't want to bring him up again, didn't want to hear them calling him a traitor, and listing the awful things he'd had to do. But he'd done those things for them, I was certain.

The mayor gave me a sympathetic look and turned away, heading to the far left corner of the room. "Garnet is thought to be a strengthening crystal. It inspires love and devotion," he informed me as he moved.

Fallon placed his hand on my shoulder, and I raised my left hand and brushed my fingers over the back of his palm before following.

There, I noticed a row of bookcases and a couple of tables.

"I have something I would like you to see," he went on as I trailed behind him. "I understand Dorothy documented her time here when she returned to your world."

"Look," I started, beginning to feel uneasy at how much the mayor appeared to know about me and my great grandma. I hadn't even had a decent introduction, yet he knew everything from who my grandmother was to who I was sleeping with. "I get the picture. You know far more about me than I know about you. But honestly, none of it's that important. Glinda doesn't matter. Tatiana doesn't matter. What matters is us getting to the tower."

Apparently, unmoved by what I had to say, he stopped at the table and pulled out a chair. "On the contrary, Miss Rose. Your friendship with the Good Witch and what you think of Tatiana are incredibly important. Please, sit down and let us share our knowledge. Beds have been made ready for you to rest in when we have finished. Luncheon will be brought shortly. My wife makes the very best bison cassoulet and has had it slowly roasting since dawn. As I said, you were expected."

"And tomorrow?" I asked. I hadn't mentioned where I was going or why I was there.

"And tomorrow, when the three of you are rested, you will continue on to the peak, to take the tower, and claim the

West," he explained, then turned to the guys. "Gentlemen, if you wouldn't mind..." Frank gestured toward the door.

I looked back at Fallon. Nox stood at his back, silent and watchful, but I didn't allow myself to focus on him, instead I kept my gaze trained on the silent man who had been through so much with me. I didn't want him to go, but if Frank wanted privacy, I didn't think Fallon would mind and I knew he wouldn't leave if I was unsafe.

Fallon gave me a tight-lipped smile, bowed his head, and turned away, moving toward the door. Nox followed, and the door closed behind him, leaving me alone with the mayor.

"I'm Frank, by the way," the mayor introduced himself.

I turned around to see him smiling broadly. "Ella."

"It really is a pleasure to meet you, Ella," he replied, leaving the table and moving toward the bookcase. "This shouldn't take too long, but I think it is important to ensure we have as much of the truth of the initial visit laid out before you continue on to claim your birth right."

"Why?" I queried, as he took a book from the shelf and came back to the table.

"There have been many misconceptions, and I would like to set them straight before you lay your claim to these lands. The people will thank us when they come to learn of it. None of us like to be lied to, but this has shaped the lives of so many, they deserve to know. Please sit down."

He placed the book on the table as I sat, opened it, and turned it so I could see.

The page showed a careful sketch of my house.

I didn't notice at first, too busy admiring the tiny details the artist had included, but after a few seconds I realized there were a pair of shoes hidden among the flowers growing near the front door. I looked up at him and asked, "What was she called?"

"The witch?" He sat down opposite me and clasped his hands, resting them on the table. "They each had many names. Tatiana has only changed hers twice, according to the annals. I was surprised to hear that the Witch of the South had gone back to using Glinda. But, to answer your question, her name was Magenthe at the time of her death. The few members of the community she allowed to address her informally would call her Mags."

"Why would they change their names?"

He sat back and grinned. "When you live as long as they do, I imagine the change is good."

I traced my fingers over the roof of the house on the page before me and smiled. "How long do they live?"

"How long is a thread?" he countered.

I raised my head and frowned. "They don't die?"

"Not of common ailments or age. The only way to end a witch's life is to take it yourself." His eyes met mine, and he added, "And take her power."

I turned the page to see another image. It was my great grandma Dot, in her gingham dress and shining silver slippers, with a tiny dog at her feet.

We'd never had a dog. I always wanted one, but Mom wouldn't allow it. Grandma had a shepherd, but he died when I was a teenager and she never replaced him.

I stared at the picture for a few moments. She didn't look powerful. She didn't look like anything special. She was beautiful, her dark brown curls sitting on her shoulders, a lovely smile gracing her beautiful face. But she was just a girl.

"How does that work?" I questioned.

"To the victor go the spoils," he said simply.

"But she wasn't here to make enemies. She was a kid, she

didn't mean to hurt anyone," I argued, trying to make him understand.

"She was brought here as a weapon. Whether the witches were aware of their new enemy or not is irrelevant. Dorothy was a weapon and she was used to claim the first of them the moment she arrived here," Frank explained, matter-of-factly.

The door behind me opened and I turned around to see two women enter.

"Ah," Frank murmured, pushing his chair back as he left his seat. "Ella, my wife, Francesca, and her sister Marianne."

I got up and turned to them as they crossed the room. The one in front carried a large iron pot, her sister a basket, and they each smiled and headed for the table.

"Miss Rose," the one with the pot began, as she put it down on the table. "It's an honor."

I shifted uncomfortably and looked down at the book. "Call me Ella, please."

"Is that your first name?" she asked, as her sister began to serve the cassoulet, and Frank pulled out a chair for the other.

"In Ella's world they don't change names often," he stated, placing his hand on her shoulder and moving around the table. "Sit down Marianne, let me. I hope you don't mind them joining us?"

I shook my head and watched him take wooden bowls and spoons from the basket Marianne had set down by the pot. He served first his wife then his sister-in-law.

"No, umm, where are Fallon and Nox?" I inquired.

Francesca gave me a curious look and answered, "Marianne vacated her home for the three of you. She will stay with us as long as you're here. They are eating there."

I nodded and took my seat. "Thank you. That's very kind."

Marianne smiled but didn't say anything.

"We were just discussing power transfer, sweet," Frank divulged, bringing me a dish of cassoulet.

He set it down gently and handed me a spoon, then returned to the pot to serve his own meal.

Francesca frowned. "I see. Have you discovered any new information regarding that?"

"No," he responded, taking the seat opposite me. "Tell me, Ella, when did you first realize you had inherited the witch's gifts?"

I'd just taken a spoonful of my lunch and was chewing on a very tender piece of meat when he asked and wasn't able to answer.

Placing my hand in front of my mouth, I set down my spoon and tried to chew more quickly.

Marianne got up and reached into the basket, retrieving a bottle of something pink and a stack of wooden cups. "Drink, Miss," she said, hastily pouring.

I took the cup gratefully and gulped a mouthful. It was the strangest thing. It hadn't fizzed or bubbled when she opened the bottle, but the liquid in my cup was carbonated. That, and very sweet. The flavor was somewhere between strawberry and watermelon, but neither one nor the other flavor was dominant.

"Sorry," I replied when my mouth was empty. "I didn't know I had until Glinda sent her steward to bring me here. I appeared at her palace wearing sparkly shoes and she told me I had to defeat her evil sister. More or less, anyway. I don't know much about these powers or how they're inherited. But they are, in my case at least, passed down through two generations."

Frank nodded thoughtfully, lowering his spoon, and Francesca nudged him with her elbow.

"Yes, dear?"

"Eat your lunch. There will be enough time for discussion later," she chided, but there was a warm note in her tone.

While not being reprimanded myself, I shoved another spoonful of cassoulet in my mouth and lowered my head. The meal was eaten in silence, and I spent my time wondering what Fallon was up to.

CHAPTER 10

$\mathcal{CD}$

When we were finished, Frank led me across the street and into the nearest house.

I had to duck my head to get through the door, but once inside the ceiling was high enough for me to stand at my full height. The same was true for Fallon, but at well over six feet, not for Nox.

I found Nox lounging on a comfortable looking chaise, flipping through a book. He glanced over as I stepped into the room, narrowly avoiding hitting my head on the door-frame, and he quipped, "You survived, I see."

I smiled and sat on a pouf opposite Nox. "It was really interesting, actually. Frank updated his notes based on my grandma's version of events, and between us we managed to decipher what really went on."

Fallon sat on the floor by my side and I reached out a hand to play with the hair at the back of his neck.

"Was it very different from what we always thought?" Nox asked, with a small line forming between his brows as he watched me reach for Fallon.

I shook my head. "No. Not from what I can tell. Only my

grandma thought the little folk were in awe of Glinda like she was. She didn't realize they were terrified and they were behaving that way to stroke the crazy bitch's ego."

"I think terrified is a bit of a stretch. They know how to keep her happy. Belittling themselves is a small price to pay for keeping their heads," Nox corrected.

"She'd take off their heads?" I gasped. "I thought that was just what they did for treasonous stewards."

He shook his head. "Mags did. She sat up there in her tower, having the villagers bringing her gifts of food and clothing to keep her sweet. Now and then she'd come down and remind them how powerful she was. That's what was happening when your grandmother landed on her. She'd take them out to the bridge and was leaning them over the side, taking their heads with a sword. Their blood ran into the river, less of a mess," Nix explained dryly.

I glanced at Fallon. He looked so sad. "How often did that happen?"

Nox shrugged. "It hasn't happened since your great grandmother put an end to her."

"But Glinda took over. What did she do?" I pressed, feeling like I had to squeeze information out of him.

"She's taken care of them, and they've sent their gifts to her. The little folk are an innovative people. Very good with their hands and they have inquisitive minds. Anything new they created went to her. Then she came and took the most skilled to live in her lands. They went gladly, knowing if they were already in the South, there would be little need for her to travel west. They keep the road between here and the Opal Palace in good condition and send their carts weekly."

I frowned. "Frank didn't mention this."

"Why would he?"

I shrugged. "He's been telling me how Glinda is the

villain, but hasn't shared the details of this agreement at all. How am I to know he isn't on her side and this is all a plan to expose my agreement with Tatiana? What if this is all a double cross?"

Nox laughed, his deep voice rumbling in his chest. "Glinda knows everything there is to know about you from her steward. What benefit would it be to them to double cross you?"

Fallon sighed and got up. He looked angry.

"What?" I asked, as he turned and left the room.

Nox watched him leave with a smirk on his face.

"What the hell is your problem?" I hissed, leaning forward slightly. "You have no proof of any of that. You can keep spouting your rhetoric, Nox, but Fallon knows him better than you do. I know him better than you do."

He closed the book and placed it on the floor, but didn't move from the chaise. "You know what he wanted you to know. You saw what she wanted you to see. You were smart enough to see through some of it, Ella, but she really caught you with him. You're compromised."

I got to my feet, balling my hands into fists and sticking them on my hips. "If that's true, why are you still here?" I challenged. He kept commenting about Sayer, challenging my belief in him, so if Nox thought I was so incapable of reading people, then why was he aiding me on my quest?

He didn't answer. I glared at him, waiting for some sort of response, but none came.

Several moments passed and my anger abated, giving way to the frustration I was feeling with the man. I couldn't tell where I was with him. One second he's saving my ass and helping me master my magic, the next he's making me second guess every decision I'd made since I got there. Not to mention I was still struggling with my attraction to him, which just added to the pile. "Seems you need to make up your mind. Either you're with me or against me."

He got up from the chaise without a word and strode toward the door, canting his head to the side to avoid hitting it on the ceiling.

I watched him go. I didn't want to fight, but I wouldn't listen to any more nasty comments he had to say about Sayer. The grudge he held ran deep, but it wasn't my problem. I had a mountain to climb, a witch who wanted me dead, and a damned war to win.

The door slammed and I closed my eyes, running my hands over my hair.

"Fuck, he's annoying." I muttered, thinking I was alone.

"Am I really?"

I turned quickly, my eyes meeting his thighs. "I thought you'd left," I mumbled, turning away.

"I was about to, but Fallon was out there listening. He left."

"Why?"

He sat back on the chaise facing me, arms braced on his knees. "He doesn't like an atmosphere. When he can't communicate his opinion easily he becomes frustrated, and added to everyone else's aggravation, he finds it easier to walk away."

"How do you know that?"

"I spent some time with Fallon after... we had a disagreement over Sayer's loyalties, and then we went our separate ways and lost touch. But we were friends once. I knew him well and people don't change so much."

I looked up and met his eyes. "No?"

His brows pulled in and he muttered, "He's different."

"Is he? How would you know?"

"He murdered my people, Ella. That isn't something the Sayer I knew would do."

"None of you are the same as you were then. I'm not the person I was when I arrived here two weeks ago. But he took me to Fallon. He told him to keep me safe. I truly believe he's been working against her in as many ways as he can without risking her finding out. He's on your side, Nox. He isn't our enemy." I wouldn't share that at times I had questioned Sayer's loyalty myself, since I wanted to remain staunch in my belief that he was on our side and that he loved me.

"You're prepared to overlook genocide?" Nox challenged, his voice was deep and loud as his anger built, but he didn't frighten me. I understood him, and truth be told, I enjoyed how fiercely passionate he was about his people. I would feel the same in his position, but I didn't believe that was the truth of it.

"When I see him, I'm going to ask him what happened," I said, trying to reason with him, "and if he did kill them all, I'll deal with it on his admission."

He gave a derisive sniff and shook his head.

"What?" I snapped.

"You risk us all for him," he muttered.

"I'm not risking anyone. I'm trying to put all this right, Nox. You're the one throwing up barriers. How do you know what Sayer has been doing? How do you know what his motives have been? So far, he's shown nothing but his desire to see Oz safe. There are two sides to this and I refuse to see him as the villain without proof. We need all the allies we can get. I need to get control of that tower. I need... I don't even know beyond that. I daren't think beyond that because she could just walk up and kill me. But I'm hoping Sayer won't let her. I have to believe he's going to keep his word and help me because the alternative—"

A lump had formed in my throat and I couldn't finish. I couldn't think about it. I didn't want to die. I didn't ask for any of this to happen, but I'd tried to do the right thing. Their world wasn't my problem. I could have just taken myself home, but I was trying to be a good person, trying to make amends for my family. I agreed to help, but I couldn't do it all on my own. I needed them. All of them, and more if they would join me.

Nox watched me for a few seconds. It made me uncomfortable, but I stayed where I was, trying not to succumb to the tears pricking my eyes.

"You truly believe he's with us?" he asked.

I nodded but didn't risk trying to speak. I couldn't hold it together that well.

He sighed. "If you're certain, then I'll follow your lead. But if he puts a single foot wrong, Ella, I won't hold back," he warned.

"I know how ridiculous it all seems," I admitted, my voice barely more than a whisper. "I don't understand it myself. But I do trust him. The same way I trust Fallon. I trust you."

I glanced up to see him smiling at me. "It isn't ridiculous. It makes its own kind of sense. I don't know why you've decided to help us, but we're grateful. All of us." There was a warmness to his tone and his gaze I hadn't seen before, and it gave me a fluttering feeling low in my belly.

Before I could respond he rose and made for the door. "I'll see if I can find Fallon."

I nodded but didn't say anything, waiting for the door to close. When it did, I left the sitting room and ventured upstairs. I needed to lie down.

* * *

MARIANNE STOPPED by at sundown with a basket slung over her arm.

"You shouldn't have gone to all this trouble," I told her as she stepped inside.

"Nonsense. It's only a few pies, and it's the least we can do," she replied, heading directly into the kitchen and unpacking her basket.

The worktops were at a height she could easily work at, but the utensils and pots I could see were the same size as any I would use. The kettle, hanging on a hook in the large fireplace to the left, was considerably larger than one I would use. "It's an honor to host the heir of Dorothy. We owe your great grandmother a great debt," she declared, making my eyebrows raise in surprise.

Fallon followed us and she glanced up. "Is Nox here still?" She waited for the answering nod. "Good. You two go wash up. Don't look like that, I saw you out by the stream a couple of hours ago. You never were much of a fisherman, but after messing with worms you need to get those hands washed."

Fallon's cheeks colored and I had to hold in a laugh. Seeing him, the man I knew would stand up to any foe without hesitation, shuffle from a room after being repri-manded by a woman who was no more than three feet ten inches tall, was hilarious.

"They don't learn," she mumbled, as she turned and pulled a stack of plates from the cupboard behind her.

"Do you know them well?" I inquired as she continued to bustle around the kitchen.

"Well enough. Nox is a regular visitor, and I've seen

Fallon a few times over the last few years. He keeps to himself, usually."

She stacked a selection of pies on a plate and returned to her basket. "Nox stops by every other week. He prowls in at dusk when the wagons leave for the palace and is out before dawn."

"What does he do here?" I queried, as she took two bottles of the pink drink I'd had earlier out and placed them on the table.

"Takes food and clothing to the unfortunates in the forest. We have to be careful, and we can't spare much without attracting attention from the South, but it all helps."

"Giving away my secrets now, Marianne?" Nox's deep voice chimed in. I didn't know how long he'd been listening to us, but he'd clearly heard much of what she'd said.

It was her turn to blush. "Phooey. Ellana is our friend."

Nox leaned over the table and snatched up a pie. "What is it today?"

"Game. Sit down and use a plate, you brute," she scolded.

I laughed and took a seat while Nox remained standing.

"You know I can't get my knees under these tables, Mari."

She smirked. "But it's so much fun watching you try."

Nox couldn't respond, his mouth was full of pie, and I snorted as Fallon returned from washing his hands.

Marianne had just finished unloading her basket and the spread was impressive. There were potatoes and fruits, cakes and salad. "This looks lovely, thank you," I said, taking a free plate and helping myself to a pie. "Will you join us?"

Marianne shook her head and picked up her empty basket. "Francesca has dinner ready. We'll all be there to see you off in the morning. Leave the dishes, I'll see to them tomorrow. You concentrate on getting a good night's sleep."

Fallon nodded to her as she moved around the table, then took a plate.

She smiled at him and I got up to see her out.

"Sit. Eat. I know my way. Good night, Ellana. And thank you, for everything."

I frowned after her, wondering what the hell she had to thank me for. I hadn't done anything yet.

"What's wrong?" Nox asked, taking a bottle from the table and drinking from it.

"You're gross," I groused, before taking a knife and cutting my pie into four smaller pieces. "And to answer your question, I'm not comfortable being thanked for something I haven't done."

He shrugged. "She isn't thanking you for anything you haven't done. She's thanking you for caring. For being here. For trying. Your great grandmother wasn't old enough to understand, but she did make a difference. For the people in the West, her arrival here improved their lives."

"Hardly," I scoffed, thinking of every other person I'd met so far.

Nox had taken a third and final mouthful of his pie. He washed it down with more pink juice then explained, "Glinda needs these people to keep her in the lifestyle to which she has become accustomed. It suits her to have an amicable relationship with them. She doesn't hurt them. She doesn't need to."

"So the threat of her becoming like her sister is enough?"

Nox tipped his head to the side and popped a whole roasted potato into his mouth. I glanced to Fallon, who nodded his agreement, and sighed. "Okay. So how do we handle the mountain?"

Fallon used two fingers to signal walking and I laughed. "Okay, smart ass. Wouldn't it be quicker if I used a breeze to get us up there?"

Nox shook his head. "No. I expect Glinda to be watching and she has little idea what you're capable of. Give her nothing. If she doesn't know you can launch an aggressive attack or escape quickly, then you have the advantage. That advantage needs to be kept quiet for as long as possible," he directed, and I didn't argue.

I pushed my plate away, suddenly not very hungry, and Fallon placed a finger under my chin and turned my head toward him. I looked up at his face and pressed my lips together.

He shook his head.

"I can't help it."

He ran his thumb over my cheek and smiled.

"I won't let any harm come to you. While I can stand, she won't touch you, Ella, and Fallon rarely misses," Nox commented, easily picking up on our silent conversation and my emotional turmoil. "Focus on claiming the tower. We'll watch your back."

I was still looking at Fallon, and I saw his eyes flick up to Nox. His expression changed briefly. I'd seen it before between him and Sayer, an understanding, an agreement. He trusted Nox.

I could trust them. We were a team.

CHAPTER 11

The steps zigzagged up the northwestern side of the mountain and it took over an hour to reach the top. The steps, hewn into the mountainside, had worn in places, making the climb hard. Fallon led the way. Nox found it easier to climb than I did, and I was forced to let him go first and pull me up several times.

When we finally reached the summit, I expected a breathtaking view, and I wasn't disappointed.

The steps brought us to the top facing east and we had an unimpeded view of the lands we'd traversed.

I could clearly see the forest surrounding the town far below. The trees closest were lush and green, gradually changing as the lands of the East merged with those of the North. The dead forest looked even more forlorn from up here. Its misery emphasized by the healthy trees that came first.

The dark, decrepit wood stretched as far as I could see, my own lands too far away to glimpse.

To the southwest were rolling hillsides, and there, in the distance, I could make out the ruins of the city.

Off to my right was the tower. I hadn't appreciated just how large the mountain was. Its flat top was big enough to house a city, and the tower was set back a fair way on the north side.

It was a strange structure, looking more like a badly stacked wedding cake than a tower, but it was beautiful in its way.

Where the Ruby Fortress was a stronghold, this was more like Glinda's Opal Palace. It was created for beauty rather than defensive capability.

Made of quartz, it gleamed in the late afternoon light. It consisted of three towers, and the structure appeared to be perfectly smooth with no hard edges to be seen. The domed roof of the tallest tower caught the sunlight, making it look just like a fountain that had frozen mid flow in winter, the cascading effect finishing the building beautifully.

"At least there wasn't an army up here waiting for me," I quipped, as Fallon put his arm around my shoulders.

"Don't bank on it," Nox muttered, as Fallon pulled me close.

I looked his way to see him scanning the sky. "What do you mean?"

"I mean," he began as he started stalking forward, "that I expected more."

"More what?" I pressed as Fallon followed, taking me with him. "Maybe she thinks—"

"Have you already forgotten the wolves? I have every confidence they were sent for our archer here. She wants you at a disadvantage. She expects you to do her bidding and hand her the kingdoms. Whether she knows he's still alive is irrelevant, her traps will have been set well in advance and have all eventualities considered," Nox warned, his tone serious as he scanned the area around us.

"Even you?" I challenged, as we caught up to him. Fallon dropped his arm from around my shoulder and fell back. I glanced over my shoulder to see him nocking an arrow.

"If she does know about me, she'll try to kill me first. You can use that time to ensure you hold the tower."

My chest tightened.

He was a reluctant ally much of the time, but he'd been as loyal as Fallon in the few days I'd known him. He'd trusted me, despite the threat I posed. But then the threat of Glinda killing me and taking the East and West was far worse. Not only that, but he'd shared my story, my truth. He'd tried to gain me more allies. "I won't let her hurt you."

The tower grew larger as we approached. I hadn't appreciated the size of the thing. Nox seemed to be heading right, looping around the building, and we continued to trail behind him. "She doesn't get her hands dirty, Ella. It'll be your estranged lover who lights me up."

I don't know what I was more offended by, him addressing Sayer as my estranged lover or that he seemed unconcerned that someone would try to kill him. After a few steps I concluded it was the former and quickened my pace.

Fallon gripped my hand tighter and pulled me back. I looked at him as he gave a stern shake of his head, indicating I needed to let it go.

He was right, it wasn't the time to argue Sayer's loyalties. That was a problem I'd have to solve later. Instead I asked, "How are we supposed to get in?"

"There's a staircase running around the outside," Nox replied as we drew closer. "It leads up to a single door... there." He pointed, and I followed his hand, looking in the direction he indicated, and saw the door.

"And it's just open?"

"It should be. If not, you'll have to figure out how to open it. From that point, you can go up to the observatory or down into the living quarters. You need the ob—"

"How do you know so much about it?" I cut him off, realizing he knew some very detailed information about the tower.

He looked at me and wiggled his eyebrows.

"You broke in?"

He shrugged. "More like took advantage of an unlocked door. The owner of the place really should be more careful. Security here is lax, to say the least."

I gave him the side-eye and murmured, "Okay, and we go up?"

He nodded. "You do. Probably safer if we stay down here."

"Why?"

Fallon blew out his cheeks and splayed his fingers.

"Boom?"

Nox chuckled.

"What?"

"Safety," was all he said.

I continued to the rear of the tower. When I reached the foot of the staircase, the two of them stopped.

The stairs were made of what appeared to be white clouded glass. I knew quartz came in an array of colors, but was most commonly found in this clear or opaque form.

"Why is it made out of quartz?" I asked, before beginning my ascent.

"It holds and amplifies the bearer's intention," he answered, stepping close behind me. "The stone cleansed when Mags died. It waited for Dorothy and she never came. Nor did the next. It's standing now, waiting for your intention. Be clear in it as you climb these steps, and it'll absorb it, bolster you.

"We know who you are, Ella. It's why we're here. The tower is a key part in securing your victory. It knows what you are. Show it who you are, your intentions, and it'll bind itself to you."

He was so close I could feel his breath on the back of my neck and my skin prickled. My stomach squirmed and I knew it wasn't anything to do with anxiety.

That was the closest he'd been to me, and I longed for him to close that tiny distance still between us. I'd been fighting my attraction to him, but in this moment, I wanted to feel his breath warm on my cheek. His lips on mine.

A shiver slipped down my spine, and before I could act on the sensations awakening elsewhere, I took a step away.

Instinctively, guiltily, I turned and looked for Fallon. He gave me a half smile.

Did he know how my body had responded to Nox?

Did he care?

Was Nox aware?

I stepped forward and away from Nox's heat.

"We'll be right here. If you need us when you reach the top, you know what to do," Nox reminded me, giving me a small semblance of assurance.

I nodded but didn't look back, instead bringing my other foot onto the first of the white quartz steps.

Despite the polished appearance of the tower, the steps had been carved with grooves for grip, and it made climbing easier.

After nine steps the stairs case curved, and I reached out a hand to steady myself on the rail and turned the corner without looking down. I didn't want to see them. I didn't want to want them at my back.

I'd relied on others too much already and it wasn't fair to them.

I relied on Sayer to deliver me to the fortress safely. Fallon had saved my life at least twice. Nox had saved the two of us from the wolves.

It could be argued that I'd saved Nox from Fallon, and Fallon from his lonely existence in the ruined fortress.

But not Sayer.

He was still stuck with her. He'd left me with Fallon, knowing he would keep me safe and what had I done in return?

Not much.

But that was going to change.

I may not have done much to help the people of Oz, but I'd learned a considerable portion of their recent history.

My instinct was spot on with Glinda.

No one was that nice. No one was that kind. That sickly sweet persona, the pretty pink gowns and the girlish giggle, were as fake as my eyelashes.

Glinda was the villain.

She was cruel and dangerous.

But I wasn't a twelve-year-old girl desperate to go home. I was a grown woman with half a lifetime's experience. I knew people. I knew myself. I knew what I had to do.

The quartz was a comfortable temperature beneath my hand, warmed by the sun all day. It felt wonderful after so many cold days in that damp and miserable forest.

I rounded another bend in the staircase and glanced up. Above me was the smooth underside of the stairs I had yet to climb. Somewhere above them was the door that would lead to the next stage of the war.

* * *

THE SUN WAS low in the sky when I reached the door. I wasn't surprised to find it open.

What I was surprised by was how dark it was inside. For a building made of glass, for want of a better description, I expected it to be brighter.

Almost instantly, the walls took on the glow of the sun, and I was able to see the whole entrance hall.

It was plain with no decoration at all, consisting of only the smooth, now yellow-orange walls curving around the circular room. To my right was the beginning of a staircase leading down, to my right one leading up, as Nox had said.

I was tempted to go down, to explore the living quarters, but I didn't have time. The sun would be setting soon, and we had to get off the mountain before Glinda showed her face. And there was still the matter of whatever surprises she had planned for me.

Turning to climb the next flight of stairs, I patted the wall and murmured, "Okay, tower, let's see what you have for me."

I stepped into the observatory and immediately looked skyward. The domed roof was clear, giving me an unimpeded view of the heavens, and I stood for a few seconds just staring up.

I'd love to be here at night, watching the stars, and I wondered if they had the same ones as us.

I didn't fully understand where Oz was. Was it an alternate universe? Was it an alternate reality? I had considered several times whether it was all part of my own imagination. Whether this was an inherited psychosis, and I was as insane as my great grandmother had been. But standing here, I realized I didn't care. Back home I had a job I loved and friends I cared about, but here I had a purpose.

Purpose. That pulled me back to what I was meant to be doing.

I glanced down. The floor was opaque, still holding the yellow glow of the sun outside, and there, in the center, was a golden disc.

I stepped forward and kneeled to run my fingers over the inlaid metal. There was a pattern etched on its surface, and I followed it with my index finger.

I didn't notice the room darken as the disc began to spin. My attention was firmly fixed on the etched pattern, which was changing before my eyes. The swirling design blurred, and I blinked a few times, trying to make out the new shapes that were forming.

Eventually I managed to focus, the words forming in my mind as I scanned them. Then my concentration shattered along with the dome over my head and I screamed from the noise and shards plunging down.

It took me a second to collect my senses. I had put my hands over my head to protect myself from falling glass, but that really wasn't the real issue.

No, the biggest issue was the three headed dragon staring down at me.

There was no instinct to protect it. No desire to spare its life as I gazed up at three sets of sharp teeth. My only thought was to get the hell away from it. The problem was, my escape route lay directly behind the dragon, and I had nowhere to run with its large body blocking my path.

I didn't want to attack, but I knew the thing was here to kill me and I really had to.

The thing with the elemental magic, I'd discovered, was that it wasn't the same as the shoes. The shoes handled my desires. My wants. My needs.

The elements had to be willed. I hadn't even known the

few times I'd used the air element that I'd been using my will. It had taken a careful explanation from Nox and several attempts before I'd got it down first time, but I had succeeded and been consistent. I drew on that experience.

The speed it came together with was surprising. With a single thought the air rushed in, sweeping around the dragon, and gathering up anything in the room not held down.

All that consisted of was lots and lots of shattered quartz.

The dragon snapped at the flying glass as it rose higher, and it roared its frustration when one of its heads took a shard to the eye. But that wouldn't be enough to get me free.

According to the words I'd read at the Ruby Fortress, and the information I had, I should have an affinity with fire. With that at the forefront of my mind, I willed the air around us to heat, hoping it would do what I needed.

Filled with rage the dragon reared, searching for a way out and trying to beat its wings. But the room was too small, and the jagged edges of the broken dome above made it reluctant to climb to a higher point. I edged to the left while I kept the dragon distracted, hoping to slip away as the air in the room was becoming uncomfortably warm. I was almost there when one of the necks bent and one of the heads lowered, coming level with my face.

It was surprisingly beautiful for an oversized, three headed lizard, with it's scales shimmering and the plume of feathers on top of its head reminding me of a peacock.

But its mouth wasn't beautiful. Its brown, stained teeth had the remnants of the creature's last meal wedged between them and its breath smelled of putrid meat.

Fighting not to vomit, I stepped back and tried to clear my mind, and will my magic into being.

The air around me instantly cooled, but the dragon became frantic. I looked up, holding my focus, and watched as the shattered quartz melted before my eyes. In seconds, the white dust and clear shards became a molten orange liquid, and the many globules came together before forming a stream in the air.

Round and round the ribbon of fluid quartz moved, winding its way around the dragon. The creature's feathers curled and burst into flame, its scales providing no protection against the searing heat I created.

It spun, desperate to escape the liquid threat, and its tail flicked wildly, catching me around the back of my legs.

I landed with a bang, hitting my head, and the room turned black.

CHAPTER 12

I could hear voices. Nox was talking.

"—didn't lay a hand on her. You unleashed that beast. This was your doing, traitor."

His voice was deep. Even when he was speaking quietly it came with such a rumble it sounded like he was growling. But when he raised it? It frightened me.

"Take another step and I'll burn you alive," Sayer warned. There was an edge to his tone, suggesting that he didn't believe his threat would stop the shifter. Nox was pissed.

Nox laughed but there was no humor in it—only cold rage. "Of course you will. May as well complete the set. How many would that make it? Three thousand?"

"Two thousand eight hundred and twenty-three," Sayer spat. Then his voice softened, and he asked, "Fallon, is she awake?"

A hand, gentle but rough, stroked my cheek and I opened my eyes.

"Tell me," Sayer demanded, his voice strained.

"I'm fine," I answered, reaching for Fallon's hand. "I just need a second."

Fallon moved so his face blocked my view of the room.

"Is it dead?" I whispered.

Fallon shook his head and ran his fingers down my cheek.

"Is she here?" I inquired, my eyes widening.

He raised one shoulder and grasped my hand.

"Is he with us or not?" I whispered so only Fallon could hear me.

His jaw tensed.

I steeled myself and nodded my head once, and Fallon hauled me to my feet.

My stomach turned as I righted, my head spinning, and I held Fallon's hand tightly.

"It was left here to kill you when you took the power, Ella. I'm expected to report back. What is this?" Sayer demanded pointing to Nox.

"Nox is here to help," I replied blithely.

"He doesn't help anyone but himself," he snarled bitterly. "What were you thinking, Fallon?"

My temper flared at his tone. Fallon would have been seriously hurt by the wolves if Nox hadn't helped us. We had no reason not to trust him. Why couldn't Sayer see that? Unless Nox was an unwelcome addition, a problem in his plans. Doubt ignited in my mind, despite how hard I'd been trying to place my trust in Sayer. "We don't have time. Sayer, I need you with me. Prove you're with me, please. Whatever oath you swore to her, I need you to swear it to me. Now," I ordered.

His eyes widened in recognition of my sudden loss of faith in him. "I can't. Ella, if she finds out she'll kill me. And if I'm not there watching her and stirring up problems, you're likely to follow."

"When I go down there, she's going to try to kill me. I'm not prepared to let that happen and neither are they. If I get away, I don't know when or if I'll see you again, Sayer. Please. Just let me know you're with us—me."

Sayer just stood there staring at me as though I'd asked for his head.

"Refusal is admitting you're her enemy," Nox growled.

I heard a high-pitched whine and looked at the dragon. It was on its side with all three heads on the floor, staring directly at me. The heads were bound tightly together around their necks, and it took me a moment to realize it was a large, solid quartz collar holding them. I followed it down its necks to the chest, where the smooth stone met its torso, impaling the poor creature. It was obviously in pain and the damage was not enough to kill it, but it was more than enough to incapacitate.

Guilt pricked at me.

Footsteps drew my attention and I turned to face Sayer. He hadn't moved far before Nox had gripped him by the throat.

"Ella..." Sayer pleaded. I could have Nox release him, but it wouldn't help. I needed to know what was going on and he needed to tell me. Now.

My chest tightened. I wanted to go to him, to hold him and be held, but Nox was right. We had to play it safe. Sayer was compromised and his refusal to prove himself to me was suspicious. "Where is she?" I asked, trying to keep my voice even.

"Outside. Ella please, there isn't time—"

"What does she plan to do to her?" Nox demanded.

Fallon released my hand and stepped between us, acting

as a barrier. I couldn't see his face, but I took a step to my right and saw the expression on Sayer's.

"Fallon, you know me, you know that I'm... Ella, did you take it? Is the tower in your possession?" There was a plea in his voice that told me he was genuinely concerned for me.

"No," I lied, still wavering.

Sayer closed his eyes and sighed. "It's the only way... when you leave this place, she'll—"

"Sayer, I need you," I pleaded.

His eyes locked on mine. He held me for a second, anguish lining his brow. "You have what you want, Ella, you always have, but I have to be—"

"That's enough," Nox interrupted, tightening his grip on Sayer's throat. "Fallon, take her out. Stay up high and watch her. If Glinda moves against her, fire until your quiver is empty."

I looked from Nox to Sayer and lowered my head. This wasn't how I wanted it to happen. I didn't want Sayer hurt. I didn't want anyone hurt. I hadn't even meant to harm the dragon. And I heard what he wasn't fully able to say. *Always have.* More importantly I believed him. "Nox, let him go."

"What?"

"You heard me. Let him go."

"He's here to—"

"If I go down there without him, she'll know something's wrong. He's supposed to have me under control, you know that," I reminded him, trying to keep the desperation from my tone.

Sayer's expression surprised me. He looked hurt. "Well you are, aren't you?" Nox responded, unable to hide the bite in his tone.

Nox released him and Sayer's shoulders sagged with relief. "No. Yes. Ella, she suspects you've turned against her.

The longer we can maintain this pretense, the better your chances. You have to speak to her," Sayer urged, his face showing concern.

Fallon gripped my shoulder and I turned to him. "It's okay. Watch my back. If she starts blowing bubbles, do your best to burst them."

He looked away and I kissed his cheek.

"It's okay. I'll be back," I promised, assuring him as much as myself.

He stepped around me and stalked toward Sayer, drawing his short sword. I didn't stop him. I followed, but didn't say anything. Even Nox stepped back.

To his credit, Sayer didn't flinch. "I'm doing all I can, it has to look convincing," Sayer pleaded.

Fallon gripped his shirt, pulled him forward, and smashed him in the face with his head. Sayer stumbled as Fallon pushed him back, and Nox began to laugh.

Sayer, hands over his nose, looked directly at me, and mumbled, "Ella..."

"Save it. There isn't time," I snapped, walking past them all to the stairs. "Can one of you help that poor thing?"

I didn't look back and was halfway down the stairs to the entrance level when Sayer caught up with me.

"Ella," he said, gripping my arm.

I pulled it free and kept walking. "Did you set that thing on me?"

"She wanted it outside, waiting. It was shrouded. I left it on the roof to watch through the dome. It was expected to attack when the disc spun," he rushed out, trying to explain before Glinda could hear.

I was tempted to glance at him but managed not to. "Well, it looks like it screwed up."

"You really didn't claim it?" he countered, incredulous.

"I was busy trying not to be eaten," I growled.

He tugged me back by my shirt and pushed me into the wall. With one hand by my head, the other cupping my cheek, he warned, "If she sees the reformed quartz you impaled it with, she'll know you're lying. You can't take those sort of risks, you've come too far."

His nose was bloody, but his eyes were bright. I gazed into them and almost allowed myself to get lost in them, remembering the last time we'd been together, how much I missed him, and how I'd worried for him. "Why?"

He pulled in his brows. He looked so conflicted that my heart ached.

"Why are you keeping this up? You don't have to, not anymore. If you stay with me, you can help—"

He leaned in, his lips brushing mine, and said, "I can't. Not yet. When the time is right I will come to you, Ella. I belong with you, but not yet."

Using the heel of my hand I pushed against his chest. He willingly stepped back and bowed his head. "I'm—"

I turned and continued down the stairs, not letting him finish his sentence, and Sayer followed without a word.

The sun was setting when I stepped outside, and as tempting as it was to leave her ladyship waiting while I descended however many hundred steps to the bottom, I figured it would save time to just float down.

I didn't bother to ask Sayer's permission and swept us both up on a breeze, over the outer wall of the outdoor staircase, and down.

There was a certain amount of satisfaction in showing her that I'd mastered something. She didn't know any of what I could do. She certainly had no idea I could access the fire power I'd inherited without having claimed the tower, or that I'd had chance to practice with it well in advance of this meeting. I wasn't nearly ready, but I was better prepared than she knew and that gave me an advantage, however slight.

"Glinda," I greeted, as I brought us to a halt before her. She was wearing one of her signature gowns—a huge, pink mélange of satin and tulle, all finished off with pearls and silver balls.

She didn't bother to hide her annoyance.

"Ellana, you now possess the tower I take it?" Glinda huffed, her shoulders rising and falling as she tipped her head and blinked at me.

I pulled my lips to one side and shrugged. "Not yet. A three headed dragon thing crashed through the roof and I had to stop what I was doing to handle that."

Her eyes narrowed and she straightened. I'd caught her attention. "You handled that?"

I shrugged again. "I'm a fast learner," I replied, keeping my voice neutral.

Her eyes snapped to Sayer, tilting her head in question. If she was concerned about the blood crusted around his nose, she gave no indication.

"My lady, it seems a Wyrm found its way south and attacked. It must have seen her alone in the tower and—"

"Where is the archer?" she chirped, her voice unnaturally high and dripping in fake concern. "Surely he was there to protect you?"

"Oh yeah," I concurred, smirking. "He was there too. He's waiting up there for me." I waved my hand over my right shoulder, roughly indicating the tower. "Not sure where exactly, but I told him to keep an eye out while I came down."

Her eyes scanned the tower and I saw her top lip twitch

when she failed to locate him. "I see... well, this is awkward..."

"Is it?" I countered, slinging out a hip. "In what way?"

Glinda smiled. "The thing is, Ellana, I know you're lying. The shoes give it away."

I frowned, looking down at my feet.

"You see," she went on, "when you arrived here you were cautious. Easily alarmed. The shoes took on a color representative of your mood and told me how much of a problem you were going to be. The answer then was not much. But now... orange represents something entirely different. You've changed. You're growing in confidence. You have a newfound enthusiasm. Your new control over both the fortress and the tower—yes, I can feel the power roiling off you and know you've claimed the tower— have given you a sense of power, leaving you to believe you can accomplish something. You are determined.

"The question I must ask myself is what are you determined to do, Ellana? As of right now, you have served your purpose, and have want I want..." She looked at her nails, then to Sayer. "She is done here. Unleash the second."

I turned to him as he waved his left hand without hesitation and looked skyward.

I did the same to see a second dragon appear as though an invisible blanket had been pulled from over its head.

This one was massive. With five heads and its wings fully extended, blocking the light of the setting sun and casting a huge shadow over the three of us.

I was about to run when Sayer grabbed me, pulling me against his chest and holding me around the throat.

Glinda had backed up several steps, grinning maniacally. She seemed to like the sight of Sayer overpowering me.

"Struggle. Make it look convincing," he instructed quietly, but I didn't have to pretend. I was struggling. "Good. Listen to me. Use wind to push me away. Run for the tower. Don't use wind to flee, the dragon will catch you. Ignore her, she won't get involved until it's time to strike the final blow. She wants to watch you struggle. Make for the tower and don't stop until you reach Fallon. I'll do what I can from here."

There wasn't time to ask questions, and I raised my booted foot and stomped it down hard on Sayer's foot, flinging back my head as I did.

It worked, and he released me just as the dragon lunged forward.

I leapt to the side, throwing myself to the ground and hoping it wouldn't catch me before I made it to my feet.

There was a piercing cry from above me and the dragon turned its attention to the sky, assessing the new threat.

That distraction gave me chance to escape and I scrambled to my feet, turned, and ran.

The relief of getting away only lasted seconds.

I saw what held the dragon's attention.

"Kali!"

If she heard my desperate yell, she showed no sign, flying straight for the dragon with her front legs stretched out in front.

I ran on.

"Ella, get up here," Nox shouted, and I heard the twang of Fallon's bow.

"Now, quickly!"

I didn't think. I leapt and the air took me.

No wind. No raging gale. I simply moved through the air, climbing steadily toward the entrance to the tower.

When I was high enough, I saw them. Nox had changed

form and was about to turn and head downstairs, Fallon was on his feet with bow pulled taut, his shot aimed at the dragon.

"No, not that. Her," I yelled, reaching for the low, polished wall of the staircase and swinging myself over. "Nox, stay here. She knows I've claimed the tower somehow, I clearly can't bluff for shit, but she doesn't know about you. Kali appeared out of nowhere, and I think Sayer brought her to buy us time. I don't know how he knew about her, but she didn't get here herself. Aim for Glinda, force Sayer to defend her and give him a reason to leave."

Fallon glanced at me and moved his aim a fraction. Nox shifted back as he fired the shot.

"How does she know?"

I looked down at my feet and pressed my lips together in a grim line. "Damn shoes."

"We need to get out of here," he urged, "while the bird has the dragon occupied."

I nodded, then looked at Fallon. "Will she be okay?"

He fired another shot in answer and the dragon roared. I could hear Kali's angry shrieks and pulled myself to my feet.

"We have to get to the far edge of the mountain," I ordered.

"And risk that thing hitting us?" Nox responded, watching the huge creature thrash wildly as Kali dug her claws into a pair of its eyes.

"Yep. Move."

Without thinking, I set off downstairs, hoping the two of them were behind me.

Nox overtook me, sprinting down in his lion form twice as fast as I could run.

The sound of Fallon's arrows clattering in his now half

empty quiver told me he was on my heels and it took less time than I expected to reach the bottom.

I couldn't see much except for the dragon, but I was sure Glinda and Sayer were gone, and I led the way, the three of us rushing over the rocky mountain top to the northeastern side. "Kali, the forest!" I yelled as we passed, and I heard an answering cry. "Nox, jump off, I'll catch you."

If he disagreed, he showed no sign and didn't look back. Fallon reached for me and grasped my hand only moments before the ground ended and the sky began.

I ran. I ran and ran until my legs were moving midair, but neither I, nor Fallon, nor Nox, fell.

I fixed my attention on the forest, on a clear line where the treetops changed from lush green to lifeless grey-brown. On Tatiana's lands.

CHAPTER 13

* the forest was dark and I couldn't be sure if I set us
down where I intended. But at least we were off
the mountain.

"Whew!" Nox yelled as he shifted, turning to face Fallon
and me. "That was something."

I smirked and nudged Fallon. "I don't think he shares
your enthusiasm." I turned and looked at him. "You seemed
okay with Kali. What's so bad about my flying?"

He looked sideways at Nox, then at me, and frowned.

"More like controlled falling?" I offered.

He nodded as an apologetic smile tugged at the corners
of his mouth.

Nox laughed, loud and long as I looked up at the night
sky through the sparse branches of the trees. "Where did
Kali go? She was right behind us," I pondered, concerned.

"Did she overestimate and fly over?" Nox asked,
composing himself.

I frowned. "I don't know, but I'd rather she wasn't out in
the open. Who knows what Glinda is going to send next."

Fallon ran his hand down my back and I leaned into

him, and murmured, "Yeah. I'm sure she's fine... I suppose I should handle shelter."

Nox was looking at me, I couldn't make out his expression—it was too dark—so I pretended not to notice and looked around. "Is there anywhere near here we could—" I was interrupted by a shriek high above and my heart stopped.

"Lioneag," Nox declared, moving to my other side as another sounded farther away. "Are you expecting anyone?"

I nodded. "Tatiana said she would meet me after. She said she'd be watching."

"But not helping, I notice," he muttered.

"No..." I knew how it looked, but I understood her predicament. "She was trying to maintain the pretense a little longer. Don't suppose it matters now, since Sayer brought Kali to even the odds. Glinda will know now."

"You think he brought Kali?" he asked.

I could hear the skepticism in his voice, and I fully understood it, but I knew it was him. "Yeah. I think she had him plant and disguise the dragons, but he also brought Kali to help us out. He's trying to balance the odds."

Nox made a disbelieving sound in his throat and I gazed up to Fallon. "I think he sent the wolves, too, but he knew you could handle them."

Nox cleared his throat.

"Yes, that didn't go as anyone expected, and we have you to thank for getting us out of there, but I'm pretty sure she's making him send... problems."

"Can you do something about the dark or shall I light a fire?" he inquired, changing the subject.

"Umm..." I looked around for a fallen branch, but stopped when I heard another cry, this one directly above us, and we all heard the beating of wings.

Seconds later, Kali crashed through the trees, breaking branches as she came, and landed right in front of us.

Turning her head, she blinked a few times and snapped her beak. Damned bird. I hadn't been exactly friendly toward her, but she'd come to save my ass anyway. I rushed forward, leaving Fallon and Nox, and wrapped my arms around her neck. She was warm, her feathers soft as I pressed my cheek into her and cooed, "That was dangerous, Kali. You could have been seriously hurt."

She clicked her beak four times and scratched at the ground, and I hugged her tighter.

"Thank you."

She made a strange piping sound, and I stepped back as another Lioneag, this one much larger, landed at her side.

"Ella, thank the wizard you're all right," Tatiana exclaimed, with no small amount of concern as she slid from her mount. I wouldn't have recognized her if she hadn't spoken, she looked so different in her armor. It looked like leather, the tunic well-fitted. The pants and boots matched perfectly, and she had swords attached to her belt.

She closed the distance between us and pulled me into a hug. "I'm so sorry you had to do that alone. Are you hurt?"

"No, I'm fine, we all are. I was just looking for a branch to make a torch when Kali arrived."

She looked down at my feet.

"Oh... yeah," I mumbled, feeling a little foolish. "I keep forgetting."

I blinked and several torches appeared around us, all burning brightly, and Tatiana grinned. "You'll pick it up soon enough. I see everything went as planned."

"If you call being attacked by Wyrms a plan," Nox muttered.

Tatiana shrugged and looked at Kali. "Did she defy your orders?"

I shook my head. "No. Sayer brought her to me."

"He needs to be careful," she cautioned with a concerned frown.

"She just appeared. Sayer must have positioned her there, or summoned her in or whatever it is he does, so Glinda thought she was always with me. I don't think he—"

"Shut up," Nox hissed, looking directly at Fallon. "Movement, southeast," he noted, listening and apparently sniffing the air. "It's her."

Tatiana drew her sword. "Ella, get behind me."

"And why would she do that, Tati?" Glinda sang from a few feet away. I couldn't see her, but the light from the torches obscured my view. Luckily, Fallon knew precisely where her voice had come from and fired an arrow in her direction.

"Tsk, not very friendly, Fallon," Glinda scolded, then ordered, "Sayer, relieve him of his weapons."

I stepped in front of him and raised a hand. "Leave him alone."

Her girlish giggle made the hair on my neck stand on end and I felt rage stir in my chest. "Have the roles reversed, Fallon? You see, Sayer? I told you he wasn't a committed pillow biter. He was never worthy of your attention."

I looked back at Fallon. He was frowning in confusion but hadn't lowered his bow.

Sayer's attack never came.

"What do you want, Glinda?" I asked, turning the subject away from whatever lie Sayer had told her about him and Fallon. "Come out and speak to me properly, you damn coward."

That seemed to do the trick.

Sayer came first. He strolled from the darkness as though he were joining us for a picnic and took us all in.

"Hello, Sayer," Tatiana greeted pleasantly. "Bree sends her regards."

His lip twitched in irritation at that name as he replied, "Tell her to keep them."

Glinda giggled again and I was forced to grit my teeth.

"Sayer," she chided, "she is still your sister."

He inclined his head and looked at me. "She is no sister of mine. Apologies, my lady, it appears Miss Rose escaped unscathed."

She stepped into the light, and the silver beads on her gown glinted as she passed the flames and placed her hand on his shoulder. "That will be short lived. Now, Ellana, you seem to have something that belongs to me in your possession. Give it up, do not resist me, and none of your friends will be harmed. You have my word."

She took three steps forward and Fallon loosed his arrow. It missed her by a mile, embedding in the tree she had stepped away from, but the warning was clear.

Kali seemed to think the witch was too close and moved between us, rearing up and beating her wings.

Tati said something under her breath and her mount joined Kali, the two of them forming a noisy barrier between us and them.

"Ella, I can distract her while you make your escape," Tatiana offered.

I shook my head. "No. I'm not running. She wants a fight, so I'll give her one."

"You can't beat her, not here," Nox warned. "She wouldn't have shown herself if she didn't have something up her sleeve. Safer to retreat now and plan your attack."

"He's right," Tatiana agreed. "Go, I'll keep her busy."

"I'm not leaving you here," I argued, as Fallon drew his bow. "She just threatened to kill me. I'm not letting that slide."

Tatiana didn't get chance to respond as the torches spurted, their flames shooting many feet in the air before extinguishing entirely.

The Lioneag startled, the one Tatiana had arrived on taking flight. Kali, however, was furious. She opened her wings full span, and I was almost certain she intended to attack.

"Kali, no," I demanded sternly, before she could act. I'd seen her go after Sayer before, and that was when he wasn't a threat to either of us. I'd hate to see what she would do to his face now. "Bring that one back," I instructed, pointing in the direction the other Lioneag had flown to get her away from Sayer.

The look she gave me said a thousand words, but however reluctant she was, she did as I said and took off after it.

I glanced around our group. Nox was gone. As was Glinda and Sayer.

Tatiana stood on my left, both swords now drawn, while Fallon remained perfectly still, his bow straining.

"You're outnumbered, Glinda," I called, scanning the darkness. "And you have no idea who else was waiting for me."

"The refugees?" she replied, her voice saccharine sweet. "What could they possibly do against me? Their flesh will be seared from their bones the moment Sayer senses their presence. Isn't that right, my sweet?"

Her sweet? Fallon had told me he wasn't screwing her, so what was that? Baiting me? Did she suspect Sayer?

I glanced over to Sayer. He'd squared his jaw and was looking at me as though to begging me not to react.

I rolled my eyes. "Okay, we'll do this your way. Can someone make sure it's noted that I tried to be diplomatic?"

"What are you doing?" Tatiana whispered.

I ignored her. Instead, I drew on what I'd learned with Nox and focused on the tree I presumed Sayer was standing behind.

It burst into flames instantly, and I heard Sayer curse. Then the heavens opened.

"Fire won't work," Tatiana commented, pulling me back by the shoulder. "All that's likely to happen is you'll burn half the forest and exhaust yourself."

"We have to do something," I argued.

Yes," she agreed. "But a standoff here isn't it. We should—"

The roar of flames cut her off, and she pulled me to the ground as she turned away from the conflagration. The sudden brightness affected my eyes and I squeezed them shut to clear away the flashing lights.

"Son of a... what the hell, Sayer?" I hissed, landing with a thud. He'd sent out a fan of flames to disorient us and it damn well worked.

I immediately rolled onto my back, looking wildly around for Fallon.

As my eyes acclimatized, aided by a lot of blinking, I made out his shape only a few feet away and pushed myself up so I could scramble to him.

He was hissing through his teeth, pressing his hands against his face, and I held him by the shoulders as I tried to check him over. But it was impossible with him holding his face.

"He's hurt," I told Tatiana when she joined me, "you

need to get him to someone who can help, where are the Lioneag?"

"I won't leave you to face her alone," she countered, looking around us.

"I'm not alone. Nox is still here somewhere, please. Help him." I couldn't keep from choking on my words. Seeing him like this, in so much pain he was making noises, filled me with fear. It was bad, and there were no medics in Oz as far as I knew. "Please. I'll follow."

Joining her index finger and thumb, she pushed the two digits into her mouth and let out a loud whistle.

I leaned close to Fallon's face and whispered, "I'll follow you, I promise," then pushed myself to my feet.

"Glinda!" My voice was hoarse with emotion, but my footsteps were sure and steady as I strode toward the tree beside the one I'd ignited, and said, "If you aren't running, you should be."

I reached the tree and kept walking with my hands by my sides. The wind was already building without me willing it to do so, the empty boughs above me creaking as they swayed, and I glanced from left to right.

"If you make it to Sayer and run along home, you're only going to have to face me later. And you won't like that. I'm alone now. I won't be next time."

"Treacherous little whore," Glinda hissed somewhere to my right. "First, I gave you power and you think you can use it against me? Then, you take Fallon's attention—he was supposed to leave, not be enraptured by some idiotic slut!"

I didn't fall for it. I kept stalking forward, listening carefully. Eventually, I heard it, the soft "pfft" sound, and I stopped. "You call me a whore, but I haven't sold myself. I gave myself freely, and Fallon did the same. Has anyone given themselves to you recently, I wonder? Has anyone declared their love for you?"

There was a rustle behind me, but I didn't look back.

"Has anyone ever loved you, Glinda? I know Dorothy thought the people here did, but I've seen something very different from the image you presented to her. I know what you did and why you did it. There's nothing good about you. You're wicked to the core."

The rain began to fall harder, the droplets so fast and cold they felt as though they were slicing my skin. My shirt was plastered to my body, my hair coming loose around my face, and I turned on the spot, my arms outstretched. "Take your best shot," I prodded as our eyes met.

She was perfectly dry, her gown unruffled and her hair set in a perfect yellow bob. "You are deluded if you believe you are a match for me, little girl," she snarled, all pretense of the pastry puff gone.

"No," I said simply, raising my hand. Her eyes locked on my fingers, on the flaming tips I was admiring. "But I'm pretty sure Nox is a match for Sayer, and without him, you're at something of a disadvantage. You have water at your disposal, and after his little display, I know that with him you have fire, but take Sayer out of the equation and you're faced with fire and air and anger. I'm not a little girl. I'm a grown ass woman who's dealt with people like you all my goddamned life. I've done this a dozen times before, and I'm not afraid."

I eyed the sky and willed it to fall. Not rain but fire, not cold and sharp, but hot and consuming. And I brought it down on her.

I knew she would protect herself, forming one of her signature bubbles over her the instant my fire touched the earth, but that was what I needed.

There was a terrifying roar nearby, I knew immediately that it meant Nox and Sayer had crossed paths, but there was no answering sound. Not even a flash of light, and I saw a flicker of panic in her eyes. Was that her only ally defeated?

I pursued my lips and sucked in a breath, before turning up the heat. "Sounds like my guy found your guy. I wonder how that's gonna to turn out?"

The rain had stopped, and my strong wind and falling fire overpowered her contributions with very little effort. She remained in her bubble, looking as though she might run at me and scratch my eyes out.

I walked toward her. She may have felt safe in her cocoon, she may have been furious at me for double crossing her, but I had every confidence it was nothing compared to how I was feeling.

"So," I started, stopping right before her. I poked the membrane of her shield with one of my flaming fingertips and heard it hiss. Her eyes widened. "We can end this now, Glinda. You can give up. You can return to the South and never leave your lands again, or I can tear your overly made-up face off and trample it into the dirt. Your choice."

"Or we can do this my way," Sayer interjected from behind.

I turned slowly, balling my hand into a fiery fist, and faced him. I didn't want to believe it, but I could hear it in his voice. He was going to screw me over. "Don't—" I began, but I couldn't finish, the shock and disappointment brought a lump into my throat.

He sighed. "I had hoped you were smarter than this. I certainly didn't want to have to be the one to end you."

"If you do it, you take the power. Then she'll kill you," I warned.

He smiled, and despite knowing how I should feel, I still felt my stomach squirm with joy from being so close to him. I loved his smile. I'd spent the last ten days desperate to see him again. I'd been worried for him. I'd taken on the whole responsibility of defeating Glinda because of him. I trusted him.

"No. Glinda the Good is my queen. She is a goddess. It is an honor to take from you what is rightfully hers. Delivering her full power is a declaration of my love for her. My final act of worship," he declared.

"You're fucking insane," I snarled, stepping back and forgetting that Glinda's bubble was directly behind me. Unexpectedly, I passed through the gelatinous membrane, and I turned again to come face to face with Glinda and a dagger I hadn't realized she was carrying.

Then we rose. Her bubble floated gracefully skyward, through the hole in the trees, and away from Sayer and Nox.

I looked at the sharp point of the blade pointing at my throat, then up at the sky.

"So this is it?" I commented, returning my focus to her and looking directly into her eyes.

Her eyelashes were insane. I regularly wore false lashes, needed them for work, but hers were just... well, they weren't any worse than the stupid beauty spot she'd stuck to her cheek.

"Yes, Ellana, now you die," she chirped.

My lips twitched and she grinned.

"I'm glad you're able to find joy in your end, Ellana. Your death will bring peace to our lands. Freedom to our people."

My smile grew wider and I tipped my head to the side.

Her eyes widened as she realized what I'd done. But it was too late. We were too high.

She turned the dagger, holding it parallel with my throat, and irritation replaced her glee.

"Maybe next time," I quipped quietly, pulling back my head.

It was just enough for her to miss as she attempted to slice my neck, her face twisted with fury.

"You treacherous—"

I managed to wink before the flame at my feet ate through the last of the membrane holding us. We fell together, and I reached out and shoved her away from me. Where she landed was her problem. As for me, I didn't bother to try and save myself.

There was no need with my friend below to catch me.

CHAPTER 14

*F*ourteen

IF CATCHING me mid fall hurt her, Kali showed no sign. My landing was awkward, and it certainly hurt me, the jarring to my back was worrying for a couple of minutes, but I righted myself and clung on. She hadn't so much as wobbled and took off at a surprisingly high speed.

I held on tightly, burying my face in her neck to protect it from the cold night air. There was a strong wind I had nothing to do with, and it was loud in my ears as she flew.

"Ella!"

I was almost certain I could hear someone calling my name, but it couldn't be. Not at this height or moving at such speed.

Then I heard it again.

The voice was faint, but I was certain I'd heard my name being called. I didn't try to search for the owner. Kali was too high up for me to see anyone on the ground and in all honesty, I was sure I'd be blown off if I sat upright.

Lioneag, I discovered, were very, very fast fliers when they felt like it. And Kali was no exception despite her smaller than average size.

"Ella!"

I turned my head sharply to the right, and despite my fear of falling to my death I sobbed with relief.

"Where the hell were you?" I yelled over the howling wind.

Nox didn't answer. Instead, he pointed down from the Lioneag he was riding on and I sat up straighter to look.

There were few clouds, and the night sky was clear. Stars, constellations I'd never seen before, shone brightly and the moon illuminated the ground below.

The landscape was rocky, and it reminded me of the top of the mountain in the West. Not far ahead was a tall cliff face, beyond that was what I assumed to be the border hills before the impassable waste, and between the two stood a black castle.

The parapets were lit at regular intervals, but there was no obvious entrance to the building from what I could see. What was clearly visible was a winged patrol moving west, to east, and back.

I looked over to Nox. He was grinning broadly, his braids blowing behind him in the wild wind, barely holding on to his mount.

I had so many questions, but it was impossible to ask right then. Turning my attention back to the castle, I clung to Kali and hoped the patrol would just let us through.

* * *

"ELLA, THANK GOODNESS."

I was surprised to see Remi standing in the courtyard, but I was warmed by the relief in his voice.

I slid from Kali's back and stroked her head, allowing her to rub her beak against my shoulder. "Thanks for saving my ass," I said softly, stepping around her and toward my general. "Why are you here, Remi? Is everything all right?"

Remi lowered his head. "Apologies. There was growing concern for your safety as whispers left the forest and spread over the planes. Talk of wolves and other creatures sent to..."

"Only wolves," Nox corrected, stepping to my side and looking down at him. "You didn't tell me your people were so loyal, Ella."

I took a deep breath. I didn't really want to have to explain it all right then. I wanted to see Fallon, to be sure he was all right, but Remi looked concerned at the appearance of the lion shifter. "Remi, this is Nox. He found us in the forest and helped me take the West. He also defended me against Sayer and—"

"Sayer?" Remi interrupted, the wrinkles on his brow deepening. "He openly attacked you?"

I shrugged. "Something like that. It's complicated, we can't really tell what's going on with him. But, we're here now, mostly in one piece."

He lowered his head. "Fallon was taken directly upstairs. Lady Bree is tending his wounds and should be with us shortly."

"Where?" I demanded, glancing around the courtyard.

There was a large, wooden door to my left and I headed toward it.

"Ella, please. Lady Tatiana left refreshment. Let me get

you something to drink, get you warmed up, and Bree will take you to him when—"

I stopped and lowered my head, fighting back tears.

"Ella..." Nox murmured softly.

I closed my eyes as he placed his hand on my shoulder. The urge to lean into him, to seek comfort I knew Fallon would offer if he were here, was tremendous. All the times I'd felt that spark of attraction and pushed it away flashed into my mind and I held my breath.

It was only there for a second before he removed it and took a step away to my right, and assured, "He's okay. Bree's handled worse than a few singed hairs over the years. Give her time to treat him."

Time. It all came down to time and I was running out of it. Sayer had put on a good show, but he was walking the line as much as I was. Fallon was injured. Tatiana had done all she could on her own. It all came down to me.

Taking a deep breath, I blinked away the tears that were threatening to fall and strode into the castle.

The entrance hall was as you'd expect. Bare. Cold. The unwelcoming feel was only accentuated by the black stone walls that absorbed most of the light from the candles in the gothic, wrought iron chandeliers hanging above. Freezing and miserable, I passed through quickly, opening a second door and stepping into what I expected to be a drafty reception hall filled with suits of armor and imposing fireplaces.

I was pleasantly surprised.

The room was airy, with doors leading off right and left. There were no windows, but the walls were built from a different stone, this more of a pink-orange in color, and the focal point was a huge fireplace carved from what appeared to be black and white marble.

There were two large tapestries on the walls on either side, but I didn't pay them much attention.

Nox gave a low whistle behind me, and I looked back over my shoulder, inquiring, "You've never been here?"

He shook his head. "I've tried to go unnoticed for obvious reasons. Well, I did until you showed up."

Guilt stabbed at my gut. He'd remained hidden for so long, able to help so many people as a result, and after knowing me for just a few days, I'd undone everything he'd worked for.

"I'm sorry. I never meant to—" The tears welled again and I choked on my words.

He closed the distance between us but didn't touch me. "Don't ever apologize. Oz has waited years for you. The people have suffered, struggled to survive, never knowing you were out there. Never knowing you would come," he soothed.

I turned to face him. "I'm not what everyone wants me to be. She almost killed me. Sayer could have killed Fallon. I didn't know where you were or what had happened to you and when I got away, I didn't turn back for you. How can I save all these people when I couldn't keep the two who've risked their lives for me safe?"

I shivered. Whether from the cold night air chilling my bones or the thought of having lost Fallon and Nox, I didn't know, but my body trembled. I felt so alone.

When I arrived here two weeks before, I was furious. Fury became curiosity, and although I wasn't sure when I'd made the decision to follow it all through, that's exactly what I'd done. Sayer made me believe. Sayer showed me I wasn't just Ella anymore.

I was a witch of Oz.

And I was alone.

Nox looked down at me and smiled. At least a foot taller than me and twice as wide, I should have felt intimidated, but I didn't. Not when he smiled like that. I met his gentle eyes and gave him a watery smile in return. Then he stepped forward and put his arms around me.

I closed my eyes and exhaled slowly as my body relaxed, that simple act bringing a physical relief. His skin was warm, despite him having flown over in nothing but a cotton shirt and his usual shorts, and I savored the heat he gave me.

"You aren't responsible for me, or Fallon, or even Sayer," he began, his voice a low rumble in his chest. "You did all the things you should have done, and we did what we could. Every action you took brought us together here. You're safe. You're with friends. That's far more important than having ended her. Than having died for us. We can plan the next move together."

I pulled away slightly and looked up at him. "You're staying?"

His tips twitched, parting slightly.

I focused on his plump bottom lip, how the soul patch of his short beard sat perfectly groomed just below.

"I'm staying," he replied softly, raising his hand and cupping my cheek.

Something stirred in me. It washed away the anxiety and the guilt. It cleansed me. It drew me closer to him, my gaze still fixed on his mouth.

"Ella," Tatiana called, blustering into the room. "I'm sorry. I meant to be here when you arrived, but Fallon was being difficult." She paused, looking at Nox and me, smirked, then continued, "Bree forced a sleeping draft down his throat in the end. Much easier to treat him when he's still."

I turned, taking a step away from Nox. "But he's okay?"

She smiled and nodded, then gestured to a long sideboard. "He's fine. Uncomfortable, but there isn't much damage, and he should be fully healed within the week, provided he looks after his skin. Bree will make sure of it. Please, you must be hungry. Help yourselves and get warm by the fire."

Nox moved immediately, crossing the room in just a few long strides and grabbing a plate.

I followed and did the same, taking a few sandwiches with odd colored fillings and a couple of cakes.

"Please, sit down. Make yourself comfortable," Tatiana offered, gesturing toward one of the large leather sofas by the fire.

She sounded anxious, as though her lateness was somehow rude. No forced niceties, like I'd come to expect from Glinda. No sweetness or well practiced speeches. She was at home, worried about a friend, and trying to accommodate house guests she felt she'd slighted. Seeing her like that assured me she was genuine. It couldn't have been an act.

Nox wasted no time, sitting sideways with his feet up.

"Nox!" I hissed, taking the sofa at a right angle to his, sitting beside the fire.

"Honestly, it's fine," Tatiana assured me, filling three goblets from a jug beside the food and handing us one each. "It's Wyrm skin, so it just wipes off. I think I have some boots that should fit you, Nox. I'll go and look later."

Unable to thank her due to his mouth being full, he inclined his head and carried on eating while she sat at the opposite end of my sofa.

"What happened?" she questioned, with concern etched on her brow.

I glanced to Nox and responded, "Do you want the short version?"

"Whichever is easiest," she said, taking a sip of her drink. "The wine will help you relax, so if you'd rather wait until after a couple of goblets, I understand."

I was grateful for her compassion. And her friendship. She really had come through for us, Fallon especially, which was a pleasant surprise.

Learning it was wine spurred me to drink, and I drained the cup. "I took the tower and she had Sayer plant a dragon to attack as soon as I did. Stupid shiny disk triggered it," I explained, setting my plate down and going back to the sideboard for more wine. "I..." I didn't want to say it, but I forced myself. "I'm pretty sure the dragon died. I faced Glinda and tried to lie about having the tower, but the damn shoes gave me away." I looked down at my feet and frowned. The shoes remained the orange-yellow color they'd turned at the Tower. "Sayer revealed his second dragon, but he had a backup—he brought Kali along. Kali defended me, and we ran, the rest you saw."

I returned to the sofa with the jug of wine and my goblet, and huddled into the corner.

Nox carried on eating without saying a word.

Tatiana crossed one leg over the other and inquired, "How did you escape her?"

"Sayer was in the process of threatening to kill me. He rattled off a speech about how he would happily destroy me, take my power, and deliver his own head on a plate to Glinda. Then he backed me into her bubble. It rose, and she was going to cut my throat, but she didn't notice me start a tiny fire at my feet. I didn't know it would work, but I panicked. I thought that was it..." I trailed off, refilling my goblet, and looked into the fire.

"And what happened to you while this was going on?" Tatiana addressed Nox, shifting her attention to give me a moment to collect myself.

He cleared his throat. "I skirted around, hoping to head Sayer off. I didn't trust him, regardless of what Ella believed he'd done back on the top of the mountain. Delivering the Lioneag wasn't enough. Not after an ambush. He professes to love her, yet he declared his love for his queen, also. But there was something..."

I closed my eyes. I didn't want to hear it. I wanted to believe he was on my side, but his intentions were never clear. They couldn't be.

Another thing was Nox's tone. For the first time since I'd met him, he sounded uncertain. As though he was suddenly questioning his own beliefs in what Sayer was and was not.

"What happened?" Tatiana pressed.

"I shifted. He had no idea I was behind him. He was watching Glinda closely, so he was easily overpowered. I was going to kill him. I had every intention of killing him, but there was something he said that stayed my paw."

I turned in my seat. "And that was?"

Nox locked eyes with me. "I don't want to say until I've substantiated his claim. But if he is telling me the truth, his allegiance to Ellana, to Oz, will be proven beyond doubt."

"What do you mean you don't want to say?" I spat. "You said—"

"I'm trying to protect you, Ella. I won't trust him without proof and I won't risk you to find out either way."

"Why?"

He squared his jaw and rose to his feet.

"Why?" I repeated, becoming irritated.

Tatiana looked at me and shook her head.

Nox turned and walked out.

I poured more wine and watched him go.

"Do you really need to ask?" Tatiana questioned when he was gone.

I looked back to the fire and didn't answer.

"You're unlike anyone they've met before," she mused. "You're sharp as a blade, yet pretty as a flower. You're selfless. Honest. Just. And now you have unrivaled power. They each came from families of note, and each lost everything at the hands of women who share some of your qualities, but not all. I, for one, wouldn't dream of claiming to be sharp, or just, or even selfless."

I looked at her and she drained her glass. "I'll have more wine brought. When you're tired, take the left door then turn right, your room is the first, Nox the second, Fallon the third. When you're ready, we'll talk some more."

"Thank you," I replied, without looking away from the fire, and she didn't say anything more.

Remi brought me wine. I said goodnight and took the wine to my assigned room. There, I found no windows, but every luxury. A large, feather bed was layered with heavy furs and thick pillows, as a fire burned in a marble fireplace with tapestries hanging on the walls.

I put down the jug and my goblet on a table by the bed and turned back to the door.

Fallon was only two doors away. Nox one. Who knew where Tatiana and Bree were? Or even Remi.

I considered checking on Fallon. I desperately wanted to see him, but I expected him to be out cold until morning.

I couldn't face Nox.

So, I climbed into bed, poured more wine, and tried to put my jumbled thoughts and feelings into some kind of order.

Top of the list was Nox. Yeah, he was hot, but that

counted for jack shit. It wasn't until he'd started really showing his colors when I felt attracted to him. He was just. He was kind. I didn't know the full extent of what he'd suffered because of Glinda, but if it was anything like what Fallon had experienced, then the fact that he managed to trust me at all was a miracle.

I tried not to act on it, because Sayer and Fallon were enough, but I had to admit that I wanted him. At least, I'd admit it to myself.

And what was going on with him and Sayer? Whatever it was, I hoped it was going to help us deal with Glinda. I wasn't close enough to Nox to ask out right, but I wanted to know what it was, and sooner rather than later. If he was staying, which he'd been certain of before, I needed to know he was fully on my side. With Fallon injured, I'd lost the advantage of having him close, for the time being at least.

Fallon. Remembering him taking the force of Sayer's fire blast brought a lump to my throat. I tried to wash it away with wine but it didn't help. With the goblet empty, I shuffled down the bed and tugged the comforter over my shoulder.

Had Sayer meant to hurt him, or was it an unfortunate accident? I doubted I'd ever know.

Exhausted, I closed my eyes and willed sleep to claim me. Tomorrow was another busy day, I had no doubt.

CHAPTER 15

Fires burned in every room in the castle, but still I felt cold.

For the first time in my life I dressed in fleece lined pants, a tank top, and a thick sweater. My boots were the sturdy Martens, but now they were lined with soft fur. Winters could be cold in Kansas, but the wind here in the North of Oz chilled me to the bone, and I couldn't seem to get warm.

I was huddled by the fire in the room assigned to Fallon when Bree came in.

"Good morning. Did you sleep well?"

I gave her a weak smile and looked over at the bed.

"He's all right," she promised, patting me on the shoulder and heading over to the bed. "To be perfectly honest, I think he's milking it."

I laughed. "You're Sayer's sister." There was no need to make it a question, the resemblance was uncanny.

She smiled sadly. "Yes, I was supposed to go with Glinda but he took my place, acting as a double agent for her."

"While you were looking after Fallon," I added, confirming the information I had gathered.

"Hmm. I hoped not to have to again, but here we are."

I could have sworn I saw Fallon's brow pull in.

"Is he really going to be okay?" I asked, moving around the bed for a better look at him. He was missing a lot of hair, and his skin was very red on the right side of his face, but there didn't seem to be any blistering.

Bree nodded. "Oh yes. Once I had cleaned it up and applied a salve, it was a simple case of him allowing his body to do what it does best. All we have now is Fallon buying himself tea and sympathy."

She poked him painfully in the side and laughed as Fallon rolled over, pushing her hand away.

She turned and began arranging several pots on the nightstand, while I sat on the edge of the bed and reached for his hand.

"How are you, really?" I inquired.

"Ah! You know the rules, Fallon," Bree snapped, dropping a piece of paper and what appeared to be a lump of charcoal on the bed beside him. "If you want people to speak to you, you must give a reply."

He ground his teeth, took the paper, and scribbled a response.

She picked it up and smirked. "Yes, I had noticed."

I frowned and peered at the paper.

He winked at me then wrote something else, handing the paper to Bree.

"You're welcome. Breakfast will be ready in an hour. Wash, dress, and be on time. The salve should be applied sparingly and only to the affected area."

Glancing at me and smiling, she turned and made for the door.

She'd barely stepped through it when Fallon pulled me down on the bed and pinned me beneath him.

"Is it very painful?" I asked, looking up at his face.

His response was to kiss me.

There was so much said in his kiss. I felt it all. In the featherlight touch of his fingers as he brushed them down my neck.

His kiss grew more urgent, and he moved his body over mine, sliding his hands beneath my sweater.

All he was wearing was pair of undershorts, and I could feel everything through them. He was hard. The problem was I was incredibly overdressed.

His hands slid up my body as he kissed down the column of my throat. His beard was soft against my skin, the soothing scent of lavender enveloping me as my body responded to his touch. My sweater inched up my stomach as his kisses returned to my lips.

"What if someone walks in?" I murmured, conscious of Bree wandering around the place.

His response was to run a finger along the waistband of my leggings.

I sucked in a breath, flattening my stomach and he splayed his hand, sliding it under the thick fabric and down over my hips. The leggings were tight, but he was determined, and his fingers soon reached my pussy.

I shifted my hips as he rubbed my clit, his tongue tickling my bottom lip as he continued to kiss me. And I was undone. I stroked his back, running my hands up to his shoulders and into his hair. Withdrawing his hand from my pants, he pushed up from the bed and my hands fell on either side of my head. He looked down at me and I looked right back, the blazing expression in his eyes igniting a fire in my veins. He moved quickly then, tugging at my pants, and pulling them down to my ankles.

I kicked off my shoes, wriggling and kicking out of them as he reached for my sweater. He didn't remove it, only pushed it as far as he could, forcing my bra up with it. When both my breasts were free, he lowered himself, sucking and licking at my nipple until it hardened. His erection was firm against my thigh, and I reached for him, sliding my hand into his underpants. I needed to touch him. To reciprocate.

I stroked his shaft and he found my pussy, sliding a finger inside. I groaned when he added another, hooked them, and began to massage the sensitive spot inside.

Turning my face away, I buried it into his shoulder, gasping as his thumb flicked over my clit, tugging me toward an orgasm.

I tightened my hand around his cock, not breaking my rhythm despite what he was doing to me and sucked in a breath as I came.

"Shhhh... Oh god..."

His mouth was on mine, and he withdrew his fingers, kissing me hard as he shifted positions. I parted my legs farther to accommodate him. With one hand in my hair, he tilted my head back and kissed the hollow of my throat before his cock brushed against me.

My breathing hitched, and whatever control he hoped to maintain snapped.

Fingers tightening, he tugged at my hair as he thrust deep and my blood sang in my veins.

He was here. He was safe. He was mine and I was his.

I had my hands on his chest and I could feel his beating heart, his skin soft and warm, as the mat of hair tickled the pads of my fingers.

And still, he kissed me—my neck, my mouth, he was

everywhere—claiming me, owning every inch of me like he would have died if he'd been forced to wait any longer.

I could feel him growing more tense and reached for his face as he reached his climax, forcing him to look at me. Making him meet my gaze as he clenched his jaw and his orgasm burst from him in a series of hard thrusts.

His movements slowed. His eyes softened, his lips moved, and while he didn't make a sound, I saw clearly what he said.

Then he collapsed on my chest with his head over my thundering heart, his breathing ragged, and I stroked the side of his face. "I love you too."

After a minute he moved to lay at my side and wrapped his arm around my waist. We rested in languid comfort for a while, prolonging the closeness.

I wanted to stay here, to not move, but I had to use the bathroom. He watched me, propping his head on one hand as I gathered my pants and shoes, with a small smile playing at the corner of his mouth.

"Don't move," I stated, ducking into the small room off the left side of the bed.

With the door closed behind me, I dropped my things on the floor and quickly dealt with my needs. When I was done, I washed, dressed, and looked at myself in the mirror.

I looked like hell. Hell, with a faint blush to my cheeks.

I smirked. Had that just happened?

Had we really made that declaration to one another?

A small thrill tugged deep in my gut. Yes, we'd said it. It was official.

It was a damn mess considering Sayer, but I knew we could work it out.

Fallon was waiting for me, and he pulled back the sheets as I approached his bed. I sank into the mattress at his side gladly, grinning when he pulled me into his arms and kissed the end of my nose.

I watched him grow sleepy and eventually, I watched him sleep. I studied every tiny detail of his face and wondered how in the world, against all the odds we faced, we'd found each other. I'd win this stupid war just to spend my life with him.

And Sayer.

Did Fallon feel the same? Was loving him the end of whatever I'd had with Sayer?

And what about Nox?

Running my fingers up and down Fallon's arm, I thought of our new ally. How he'd come to our aid. How he'd helped me for no other reason than he wanted to.

He saw something in me that was enough for him to risk everything, and I wondered why that was. Why he smiled at me the way he did. How he laughed. The way his lips twitched with amusement at the little things I said.

He was staying. Those were his own words, and his actions spoke much louder. If Tatiana hadn't stormed into he room like she had, I knew he would have kissed me. I knew that I'd have let him. That I'd have kissed him back.

I pondered how his braids would feel beneath my hands and how his full lips would feel against my own.

I caught myself as my mind trailed over the rest of him and quickly pushed him from my mind. It was the wrong time.

I was there to help people, not to claim half the male population for myself. What the hell was wrong with me?

CHAPTER 16

Fallon was still asleep. I had so many things to do and I knew I should go find Tatiana, but I was finally warm. I was relaxed. I was content to just be here with Fallon, with his arm circling my waist, listening to his breathing.

I carefully slid from beneath the sheets, hoping not to wake him. Once my shoes were on my feet I moved over to the fire, dropping a fresh log in the grate. I didn't want his room to cool down and wake him. He needed the rest. I needed him to recover. I needed him with me through what was to come, I couldn't do it alone.

Bree was in the sitting room with a pot of tea and plate of cookies. There was no sign of Nox.

"Please, join me," she offered, pouring me a cup. "Do you like it sweet?"

I nodded and sat beside her as she stirred what appeared to be a spoonful of honey into the hot liquid.

"Just you?" I asked, accepting the cup and saucer she offered.

She smiled and took her own cup before sitting back.

"Tati is at the border. The Wyrms are attacking the breeding colonies of Lioneag. She is trying to help."

"How can she help?" I queried, sipping my tea.

"She has her methods," she replied with a short laugh. "It usually ends in a new set of armor or item of furniture. Of course, those in the forest have no complaints, they must eat something."

I frowned. "How many are caring for them?"

"Several dozen. The little folk send what grain and cloth they can, Tati provides fruit, feathers, and meat, and the Pumpkinheads provide vegetables. I keep supply medicines and cleansers among the communities."

"And Glinda?" It was a stupid question given what I knew of her, but it was worth knowing for sure.

"Sends her wolves to hunt down the weakest. Those less able to run or hide. She does her best," she remarked bitterly. "Tell me, how are you adapting to life here?"

I put my saucer on the table before us and turned in my seat. "I don't think I am," I answered honestly. "It's still all like some really bad dream."

She smiled sadly. "Unfortunately, this is reality here. Tati does what she can, we all do, but the destruction her power wreaks leaves her limited as to how she can handle her sister and, in her reluctance to do too much harm, she gave Glinda the advantage."

My eyebrows rose of their own accord at her candid comment.

She saw my expression and explained, "I can and will outline her failings. I am not Sayer and she is not Glinda. In trying to do good, she did nothing, and the cost was high. She'll tell you that herself. But another reason, a deeper reason, is that she doesn't want absolute power. She never did. She chose the North because there were no people to rule."

"But she seems so well liked," I said, picking up my cup again and helping myself to a cookie. "Surely the people would rather have her than Glinda?"

Bree smiled. I could see the love she had for her mistress in her eyes as she did. "They would," she replied, "but with her family's record for tyranny with any amount of power, I think her choice was well made."

I shook my head. "That's bullshit. Your family doesn't define who you are. Being an asshole is a choice you make all on your own."

She laughed and put down her cup. "I agree. But we are influenced by those around us. I understand Dorothy suffered when she left here. I would argue that her experiences shaped the people around her. Her daughter loved her and grew up to be a compassionate, patient woman. Her daughter—"

"Is an asshole," I interjected. I didn't want her to have any misconceptions. My family had its faults just as Tatiana's and hers did.

"Yet you are more like your grandmother."

Somehow, I didn't think Grandma had this much male attention.

I shrugged. "Maybe. I tend to keep to myself, too, you know?"

"Do you really?" She sounded surprised. "Why?"

"I work a lot, and my job isn't exactly..." I took a deep breath. "I dance for men. It pays well, but there are a lot of misconceptions around the job, it's kind of taboo, you know? So, I work, I hang out at the bar where I work, sometimes have coffee with a few of the other dancers, but it's easier not to have to handle people's judgment."

"So you have no partner?" she pressed.

I thought of earlier with Fallon. Of what we shared. Not the act, but the feeling that came with it. Was he my partner? What about Sayer? I hadn't come to a conclusion about him yet and I didn't know if I were ready to.

I shook my head. "Guys like to watch me dance. They don't want other guys watching their girl dance. It's cool, I don't have an issue with that, I'm just not changing my life to fit someone else in."

"And what about Fallon?"

I looked at her sideways. "What do you mean?" I hedged.

"Not just Fallon," she said with an amused smile. "I mean, I heard my brother fell head over heels for you the second he met you. Fallon had much the same response, and the tension between you and Nox is... tangible."

Surprised by her apparent acceptance of the strange situation, I grimaced and asked, "Tatiana mentioned that, huh?"

"I heard all about you from Fallon, actually," she replied, picking up the teapot. "More tea?"

I gave her a questioning look and presented my cup.

"Keeping him still while I tended the burn was easier with him concentrating on you. He told me about your arrival at the Ruby Fortress. How you faced the inhabitants of your fortress and claimed it for your own. How you took on the responsibility of your new position, not for personal gain but out of compassion for the people.

"He told me how my brother described your instant dislike of Glinda."

"I wouldn't go that far," I clarified in mild protest. "I just can't stand pink and her voice gives me a headache."

Bree laughed, putting the teapot back on the table. "It really is a terrible affliction, that voice of hers."

"Hmm. I wondered what the world did to deserve it." I took another cookie and nibbled the edge before asking, "I still can't fully believe she's like this, my great grandmother thought she was wonderful. Has she always been so... wicked?"

She nodded her head solemnly. "I'm afraid so. She ordered the exe—"

"I heard," I interrupted, not wanting to hear the details again. It made me sick. "Nox told me. Does that mean Sayer really did... did he do it?"

"I wasn't there," she said, her voice strained, "but by all accounts, the two tribes went into the building for talks, and only Glinda and Sayer came out. Nox being the exception, of course."

And we'd come back to Nox.

I took a large bite of my cookie and looked at the tapestry on the wall. I hadn't paid much attention to it the night before, but I was suddenly incredibly interested.

It was the city. The Emerald City, my great grandmother had called it.

The palace loomed over the lower levels, with the many cylindrical towers reaching into the sky. The fields outside were full of flowers, the forest to the north a mass of healthy green. It was nothing like the wasteland I'd seen, or the decaying wood I'd walked through.

"Was it really made from emeralds?" I inquired quietly.

"No. It was a trick of the light," she said softly. "The city was sculpted from a huge prism rock by the first witch. The lower levels were just plain stone painted to match the grand towers. They're all black and grey now, a charred ruin after what Glinda and Tati did to it. Tati didn't want to. She grew up there, the city was her home and she loved every inch of it, but Glinda kept on pushing and eventually her hand was forced.

"Such a shame it came to that. It really was the most beautiful place..."

"Maybe it can be rebuilt," I suggested, looking at the rest of the woven image.

"Not until Glinda is stopped. She won't have it. Any attempt to restore the city will be met with wrath," Bree concluded, with a stern shake of her head. There was a hard edge to her tone that surprised me, and when I looked at her face, she was almost scowling up at the image.

"Why?"

"She believed the city was hers. As the eldest of the sisters it was her right, and her mother gave it to the wizard. Naturally, Glinda was incensed, but she was very careful in her planning. Who would have suspected it was she who brought a child from another world to carry out killings on her behalf? Of course, she rushed to the child after her first trap was sprung, assuring her the witch was wicked and not a loss at all, and sending her on her merry way. Her meeting the yellow mane lion was a happy coincidence. The same with the scarecrow and the woodcutter. They each played a part in her scheme. By the time Dorothy returned home, leaving the slippers behind, Glinda had set the wheels in motion. The slippers answered to no one and neither did the winged guard. Of course the fighting started, and the city was razed, but Glinda got what she wanted. She was free to claim the East. She was free to build her army and pinpoint you. She even found the perfect lure in my brother."

I turned my head sharply and pulled in my brows at the mention of Sayer. If she noticed, she showed no sign, her focus still trained on the tapestry.

"But as luck would have it, she underestimated you. Everyone did," she continued. "Sayer knew the effect you had on him, he'd been watching you for a time, hoping to find a way to avoid bringing you here. It must have pained him to hand you over to Fallon, to return to the palace when every part of him told him his place was at your side. But he believes, and Fallon believes and now Nox believes, that when all this is over you will love them regardless of what each of them must do to win this... they know they have you."

"He told you all that?"

"He didn't need to. I can see it in each of their expressions when you're mentioned," she said, turning her head toward me and smiling. "They won't let you down."

I don't know what she saw in my eyes, but she reached out and took the saucer from my hands and asked, "Why do you fight it?"

"I'm not fighting anything. Sayer isn't here and Nox..." I sighed. I didn't know if I was fighting or just avoiding, but I didn't want to answer her regardless. I'd jumped from Sayer to Fallon, it was true. And I had feelings for both of them that were confusing and not usual. The normal thing was one partner, wasn't it? That's how it always was. And now there was Nox. I didn't know what was going to happen there, but if he kept touching me the way he had yesterday, I could guess. I couldn't just split myself between three guys. Could I?

Maybe I could. I was doing okay with Fallon while Sayer was still in the mix, albeit he was absent. The real question was, did I want to discuss my private life with a complete stranger? She may have shown me nothing but warmth and welcomed me into her home, but I wasn't usually one for sharing. "There are more important things to worry about,"

I replied instead, trying to shift the turn our conversation had taken.

She patted the top of my hand and got up, taking the tea tray with her. I thought she was going to just go, but she looked back down at me and added, "Perhaps. But it can make all the difference knowing you have people you can absolutely rely on."

I pressed my lips together and nodded, and watched her take the tray and leave the room.

CHAPTER 17

Nox found me in Fallon's room.

We were sitting cross-legged on the bed, looking down at a book, the pages filled with his words. I loved looking at it, it was beautiful. The way it sloped to the right, each letter carefully connected to the next, the wide loops and spaces making each gracefully crafted word a joy to read.

I was adoring having him fully reply to my questions and had managed to coax a good amount of information from him. He'd turned the tables by writing down questions for me to answer, and when Nox walked in their eyes met in an undecipherable way.

I looked from him to Fallon, trying to figure out what was going unsaid between them, but there was nothing to tell what it was.

Then Fallon nodded his head, just once, and Nox turned directly to me and asked, "Do you have a minute?"

I glanced to Fallon for his approval. He took my hand and smiled, nodding toward the door.

"I'll be right back," I murmured, before kissing him. "Don't run off."

He gave me a half smile and I turned to leave him and found Nox gone.

"I mean it," I said, glancing back at Fallon. "I won't be long."

When I stepped into the hall, Nox was leaning on the wall opposite the door.

"What's up?" I inquired, leaving the door ajar.

"We should think about moving. We're running out of time," he stressed, giving me a meaningful look.

"We?" Part of me had expected him to take off. To go back to the West, to his life, like he had that night in the forest.

"You. Tati. Fallon. Us," he listed, looking directly into my eyes. "I'm not going anywhere, Ella. We're all affected. We're all here living this. We may not have known it, but we waited for you. We've protected you. We all have your back. But she will be moving, and if we don't move too, then she'll take the advantage."

Whatever that meant, I wouldn't allow it. We'd all come too far. "How?"

"She'll gather her forces, or more likely have Sayer do it —saves time."

Anxiety contracted my chest. That sounded like battle. We didn't have the numbers and with no way of knowing what Sayer would quite literally drop on us, we were screwed. "What forces?"

"I heard she was building an army. She has hundreds of Wyrms at her disposal at the least. You can match her easily, but if you're not prepared when she strikes, you stand to lose everything."

"Where will she attack? Here? The fortress?"

He shook his head. "No, closer to home. The city is her aim, that's what she wants as her palace—a central point she can rule from. If you get there first, if you restore the defenses, we can make our stand there."

We. He was with me every step of the way. "Why are you helping me?" I asked.

"I've watched from the shadows for years. I've done all I can with what I've had, but it wasn't ever going to be enough. Then I found you. I've watched you. The people here love you. They know you really care. I told you what happened to my people and I'd rather die fighting for what they believed in than swear fealty to her. We can't stay here, need to move."

I looked back to Fallon's door. Had he heard all that? I'd tell him everything later anyway, but I'd rather not have a conversation behind his back.

"I think this is a conversation we all need to have together."

He nodded. "Tati should be back soon. Shall we go and get lunch while we wait?"

I looked back at Fallon's door, torn between going and staying. I didn't want to leave him.

Nox chuckled. "Tell him to get himself together and we'll all go."

I didn't need to tell him anything. His door swung fully open and he stepped out wearing his usual leather pants and a black tunic. His hair was neatly combed back, and his skin glistened with a thin coating of the lavender salve Bree was using to treat his burns. It was working well, that side of his face now pink with little evidence of injury.

"Looks like he's together," I observed brightly, before turning and leading the way to the sitting room.

It was strange, but for the first time since we left the

town in the West, I felt completely at ease. Whether it was knowing we were safe for a time or just having them both close, I didn't know, but I liked the idea.

When we arrived in the sitting room there was a table set for six. There were only bowls and side plates, spoons and knives at each setting, with a large tureen and basket of bread rolls in the center of the table. Bree was sitting with her hands clasped to her chest, her eyes closed, and her lips moving quickly in a silent prayer.

I paused in the doorway, and the guys stood silently behind, while all of us let her finish.

"Thank you," she said when she opened her eyes. "I made soup. Please come and help yourselves."

"Gladly," Nox replied, barging past me and into the room. "Seems like it's been forever since breakfast."

Bree laughed. "I'll fetch more bread."

"No, no," he protested, striding straight past the table and to the door on the opposite side of the room. "I'll get them, I remember where you put them when you pulled them from the oven."

I watched him with my brows raised as he left the room.

Bree was still chuckling when I sat down beside her, and she commented, "He's wonderful company."

I glanced at Fallon as I pulled in my chair, and said, "We haven't really gotten to know him very well."

Fallon poured himself a drink from one of two jugs on the table and smirked.

"I expect that will change now," she replied, before standing and serving me first.

I looked at the empty seats. One was clearly for Tatiana, but the sixth had confused me. "Who's missing?"

"Remi," she answered, filling her own bowl. "He

returned to the fortress shortly before you arrived. I was praying for his safety."

"Why did he go so quickly?" I asked, watching her step around the table.

She paused when Fallon shook his head and gestured to her seat, then Bree smiled and sat back down.

"He called by for an update on your safety. When he received it, he returned to the fortress. I did try to persuade him to stay, but he said he was needed. Training is going well and he hopes to see you soon."

JUST AS WE were finishing lunch, Tati returned from the border. She looked awful, charred, and exhausted as she flopped into the seat beside me and sighed. Her armor clattered, and I eyed her with a frown. Bree instantly got up and served her a bowl of soup.

"Finish your lunch," she insisted. "I can—"

"You are exhausted," Bree countered. "What happened out there?"

Tatiana looked around the table. Fallon was staring at her intently, his bowl pushed far in front of him, and his arms resting on the table top. Nox was much the same, only he sat back, with one elbow resting on the carved chair arm, and fiddled with one of his braids.

"It was difficult to tell. The unrest in the Wyrm colonies is getting out of hand. The females are frantic. No sign of the males. Their instinct, when something is amiss, is to turn and attack the Lioneag colonies. I managed to send a few dozen eggs back, but many were smashed and the females are mourning over their nests."

Bree delivered the soup, stroked her hand gently over

Tatiana's hair, and kissed the top of her head. "I'm sorry, love."

It was such a small, natural gesture that it almost passed me by, but the realization that Bree and Tati were, well, Bree *and* Tati, was something of a revelation to me. I didn't even consider it, after Sayer had so vehemently denied a relationship between him and Glinda. But Tati wasn't her sister. She was kind and thoughtful. She considered others and fought for what was right. Of course Bree loved her.

Trying not to smile at the warmth filling me, I attempted to focus on the conversation.

Tati just nodded and picked up her spoon. "Nothing we can do now. I left a squadron of Lioneag there to watch the nests, what eggs I salvaged are upstairs. A few of the younger females are sitting on them. What did I miss here?"

"Not much," Bree replied, returning to her seat. "Fallon is well recovered, although he does need another few days using the salve to ensure his skin is properly healed. Nox has decided he's staying close to Ella, bringing her personal guard to two. It has been noted that Sayer is an unknown entity."

"He hasn't joined her," Tatiana stated firmly. "He's doing exactly what he said he would do. He's sacrificed more than any of us. If we doubt him now, we're certain to fail."

"We have a plan," Nox informed her. "Remi will hold the West. Ella will head south and work on the city's defenses. When the city is secure, we will move all our forces there and make our stand."

Tati nodded her agreement, and offered, "Take as many Lioneag as you need. We will need an envoy to relay this information to the East. Whether they will come is up to them, but they must be given the option to fight for their freedom."

I cleared my throat. "I'll go. Glinda won't expect me to return there, and then I can double back to the city."

"I have somewhere to go first," Nox announced. "If you can wait, two days—"

"Where?" I asked, interrupting him.

He looked around the table, then at me and shook his head once. "I can't—"

I remembered then what he'd said about Sayer. Something had changed between them, and Nox needed to look further into Sayer's claim.

Nox looked apologetic. He had something to say but I could see he wouldn't part with it here at Tatiana's table.

There was a tense silence Fallon broke by putting his glass down a little more heavily than necessary.

I looked to him. Fallon was staring at me expectantly.

"You're staying here," I ordered, looking over the table at him. "I need someone to plan around her attack. You know what she's most likely to bring, how she'll hit the city, and where. And we don't know what she has lurking out there. If she manages to track me, she'll kill everyone I'm with. Please Fallon, stay here. Let Bree finish—"

He stood abruptly and left the table, striding toward the door without looking back.

I let him go. I didn't want to get into it at the table. I had to explain and I couldn't with people here to interrupt.

I understood that he wanted to stay with me. The truth was, I didn't want to be apart from him either, but if we stayed together and Glinda found us... it wasn't worth the risk. It would be easier to sneak into the city just Nox and I. Easier still if one of us were a black cat.

I watched him go, with guilt tugging in my chest. I could tell Fallon felt rejected, but with Sayer acting as Glinda's puppet, Tatiana as Glinda's sister, and Bree compromised by her affection for each of them, I needed someone I was certain I could trust.

No one scored higher than Fallon. He was unwavering loyal. But he wasn't fully healed.

"When do we leave?" Nox questioned before he was out of the room.

I shot Nox a contemptuous look and picked up my goblet.

"That was a dick move," I snapped, knowing he said it to goad Fallon.

"Ella, this is no time—"

"You're an asshole," I muttered, knocking back my water. "Find yourself a Lioneag. I'm riding Kali." Pushing my chair out with the backs of my knees, I rose and looked to Tatiana. "Thank you for having us and for keeping Fallon here. Maybe you should find someone else to inform Frank of these latest developments, it looks like I'm going to be tied up. I'll be back as soon as I can."

She gave me a weary smile. "The legion will be battle ready in two days. Send one of your guard with news, I can come to you when you're ready."

I nodded once, then turned to Bree. "Look after him," I pleaded, knowing she would understand.

She smiled gently, and soothed, "He'll calm down. Good luck."

With a tight smile I headed out into the hall. "Fallon?"

He was halfway up the stairs, but paused when he heard me and waited.

"I'm sorry," I said, taking the stairs two at a time to catch up with him. "I need you here. If we stay together and Glinda has an ambush set, we're all screwed."

I searched his eyes, he looked so dejected. Grasping his hand, I raised it to my lips and kissed it. "Tati loves her sister.

Bree loves her brother. They love each other. I need someone not emotionally involved to keep everyone straight. And I want you to heal. God, when I saw that happen to you I—" I choked, the memory of seeing him so horribly burned taking my breath away. Reaching for his face, I stroked his cheek and continued, "I'll meet you at the city in a few days. I don't want to leave. Believe me, if I could, we would, just you and me, but I can't. I have to make this right. For you. Them. For Dorothy. This has to end, Fallon, and it's up to us. You got me this far."

His shoulders slumped, and he relaxed into my hand.

"I love you."

Reaching up on the tips of my toes I kissed him softly.

His responding kiss was slow. Tender. Reluctant somehow, as though he wasn't sure if it would be the last.

"I'll see you in the city. I have to go."

He let me pull away, and I left him on the stairs turning and heading outside.

When I reached the courtyard I paused and scanned the battlements. "Kali?"

"Ella, I need to check something out before we head to your fortress," Nox told me as he came up behind me.

I squared my jaw and turned to face him. "Giving me orders now, too?" I snapped.

He took two swift strides and was right in front of me, his chest only inches from my face. "It's worth the detour."

"Really? What could be so important?" I countered, taking a step back and looking up at him.

I expected there to be some challenge in his expression, or the usual mischievous glint in his eyes, but I was disappointed. All I saw was pleading.

"It proves one way or another if Sayer is really with her."

There was the unmistakable sound of wings at my back,

then the scrape of claws on the cobbles. I took a deep breath and turned to Kali, scanning her to find the easiest way onto her back.

Right then, another Lioneag landed beside her and I watched Nox stride forward and swing himself up onto its back just before its wing joints.

Kali lowered herself to the ground, making it easier for me to climb on, and I managed to get into the same position Nox had.

"What if it's a trap?" I asked him, while Kali turned around.

He grinned at me. "That's why I'm taking you with me. What use is having a witch if she can't watch your tail?"

I scowled as his mount took off and glanced back at the door as Kali took flight. I couldn't see clearly, but I was almost certain I saw Fallon standing just inside the entrance.

My Fallon. My love. My support.

CHAPTER 18

Leaving Fallon was hard. Necessary, but hard.

He'd been at my side since I'd arrived at the fortress. He'd protected me, loved me, and I'd repaid him by leaving him behind at the overlook.

But I had to. He wasn't fully healed after Sayer had burned him in the fight, and I didn't know if Nox was being led into a trap. I didn't know anything about where we were going, or why, but it seemed important to him. And I owed him.

Kali began the flight by fighting to take the lead over Nox's mount. When she felt comfortable with her position in front, we remained that way for hours until I leaned in close, and murmured, "Slow down. We don't know what we're heading into."

Nox noticed we'd fallen back and slowed his own. When Kali drew level, he signaled down. I had no idea where we were or how long we'd been flying, but judging by the position of the sun in the sky and the pain in my hips, it was approaching dinner time. What I did know was that he must be damn near freezing. I'd given myself a thick coat only a couple of minutes into the journey. He was only wearing a cotton shirt and leather pants, and while it was the most I'd seen him wear, I didn't know how he could stand the icy wind.

His Lioneag began its descent and Kali followed. I took the chance to scan the landscape.

The terrain was as rocky here as was it was around the overlook, but it was bordered by what appeared to be a mountain range. It seemed to form a corner, which was strange, as though Oz were a square island bordered by a rocky outcrop. The Lioneag continued their steady descent, riding the air currents toward this unnatural corner, and I searched for landmarks below I could use to navigate back to the overlook if necessary.

We finally landed in the shadow of the westernmost mountains and I slid from Kali's back the second her wings folded in.

"There's nothing here, Nox," I said, looking around.

He didn't say anything, just patted the side of his bird's neck and dismounting.

His mount had a bag clutched in the talons of its left foot, and Nox tugged it from the tight grip before turning on the spot and peering around.

"It'll be dark soon. Once the sun falls behind these rocks, the temperature will fall too. We should get comfortable," he suggested.

Kali and the other Lioneag followed him toward the natural wall, and I had no option but to join them.

"So, what, we just spend the night out here?" I asked.

He pulled a thick fur blanket from the pack and held it out to me. "Yes."

I took it and wrapped it around my shoulders before sitting with my back against a large bolder. The two Lioneag found themselves a ledge above us to perch on and appeared to settle down to sleep, while Nox sat on the ground opposite me, leaning on the pack.

"Are you going to tell me why we're here?" I inquired, suddenly questioning his decision to come out here. I tried, and failed, to keep my irritation from my voice.

He looked at me. "Are you going to tell me why you're snapping at me all of a sudden?"

"I'm not..." I trailed off. I couldn't lie. "I haven't meant to."

"I get that, but what did I do wrong? All I've ever done is trust you. I've defended you, I've joined your cause. What more do you need from me?"

He spoke casually, but I could see how he truly felt in his eyes. They were so expressive. He couldn't hide it.

I glanced down at the rocky ground and picked up a pebble. "It's complicated," I hedged, unused to speaking about my feelings.

"The relationship between you, Sayer, and Fallon? I don't see how. If they love you and you love them, and it's clear you do, there's nothing to complicate," he stated easily.

I kept my eyes on the pebble in my hand, turning it over and over.

He watched me for a few seconds before continuing, "But everything seemed fine until we were alone at the over-look. Then Bree walked in and your behavior changed. You went cold. Why?"

I didn't know why he was torturing me.

Could I sit here and admit I was attracted to him as well? Would it make things awkward?

"You don't have to answer me, but I'd appreciate it if you could give me a reason. There's no one here to hear you, and Fallon won't ever find out," he assured me, his tone gentle.

If he was trying to goad me into voicing how I'd felt in that moment he could think again.

I was in no position to be chasing a third man around Oz. And the thought of it was absurd. Three guys? Okay, so Sayer had been out of the picture longer than he was in it, but Fallon was okay with my relationship with him. That didn't mean it was okay for me to chase every guy I felt a flicker of attraction toward.

"I'm just a bit... stressed," I muttered. "I'm sorry, I shouldn't have taken it out on you."

Apparently done making me squirm, he sat upright and asked, "You hungry?"

I nodded and he reached into the pack.

"Good. Bree sent soup, but I managed to swipe some scones when I passed through the kitchen later. Sorry, the soup is probably cold."

He handed me a flask and I took it gratefully, opening up the stopper. A plume of steam escaped and I put the flask straight to my lips.

"It's still warm," he noted, surprised. "Have to say it's impressive how those women can create almost anything from a dead Wyrm."

I drank my soup quickly then handed back the flask.

Nox exchanged it for a large fruit scone and I huddled back beneath the fur to keep warm.

"Feel free to make a fire," Nox commented.

"I didn't think you felt the cold," I countered, glancing up at him. "Anyway, aren't we supposed to be keeping a low profile?"

The light was fading fast, but I saw him smile and shake his head. "No. There's nothing to hide from if Sayer's as trustworthy as you say. I'm trying to do it your way."

I didn't ask him to elaborate, and produced a small fire

between us—just big enough to keep us warm without drawing attention from far away. He may feel at ease up here in the left hand corner of nowhere, but I didn't. Every time I closed my eyes I could see the look on Glinda's face as I escaped her. She was out for my blood. I'd rather she didn't get it. Especially not out here.

"Thanks," he said, stretching out on his back and tucking his arms behind his head. "Saves me from having to shift."

"Why don't you want to shift?" I questioned, huddling farther into the fur despite the fire.

He didn't answer and I didn't push.

Instead, I sat thinking through the last few days and all that had happened.

Fallon was going to be okay. Tatiana seemed to have a plan.

I kept coming back to Nox. Was he really attracted to me the way I was to him, or was I blowing it out of proportion? He'd become distant somehow. Probably because of my own fluctuating emotions. There was so much going on I couldn't keep up, and was beginning to think I was seeing something that wasn't really there.

The fire was doing its job and I was starting to feel sleepy. Nox hadn't said anything for a while, so I leaned back against the boulder and closed my eyes.

I was almost asleep when Kali hissed, stirring me.

"Call her off," Nox whispered into my ear.

I startled, turning my head sharply toward him. "What?"

"Kali," he said, his voice a low rumble. "Now."

I noticed his hands were held up in front of him and looked around wildly. "What's happening?"

"On your feet," a strange voice ordered.

My chest contracted and flames coated my hands.

"Put it away, witch, or your friend dies."

"I..." I shook my hands, trying to extinguish the flames. "I can't."

"Ella, please. They won't hurt us if you do as they say," Nox pleaded, a warning in his tone. "Just calm down, call Kali off, and do as he says."

I looked up to the ledge where Kali and the other Lioneag were perched. Both were gazing down at us, their eyes reflecting the light of the fire. Kali looked like she was ready to eat someone. Her feathers were puffed out around her head and neck, and her claws were gripping the rock so hard it was crumbling. "Don't... just stay up there. We're fine."

I pushed myself up on my knees and looked behind me. "There. She won't attack. Who are you?"

A hand closed around my upper arm and hauled me to my feet. "Move."

I looked to Nox and when I saw he was getting to his feet without being manhandled, I fought to hold my temper. He began to move after the guy closest to him and I shrugged my arm free, muttering, "All right, pushy," then followed directly behind Nox.

Kali cried out as we moved toward the north wall, and I looked back at her, hoping she would see my expression.

She calmed right down, but didn't take her eyes from me while I stumbled into the darkness.

"How did you find us?" the guy behind me demanded.

"He brought me," I confessed, pointing to Nox. "And he was tipped off by—"

"Abel, take him down. I'll follow soon," he called to the guy ahead.

"Just do as he says, Ella," Nox ordered. There was an

edge to his voice I wasn't sure of. It didn't sound like fear. He seemed too relaxed.

"Wait here, witch," my guard said, tugging on my coat.

I stopped moving and shoved my hands into my pockets. It was cold away from the fire, and dark, and I didn't want to risk starting any fires that could cause me to lose my head. "Look, I'm not here to hurt anyone," I stated, turning to face the guy.

"Stay right there," he warned.

I didn't. I carried on turning until I was face to face with him, and I was both surprised and relieved at what I saw.

"Keep your hands where I can see them," he warned, raising an axe.

I swallowed, nodded, and brought my hands out of my pockets. "I'm not here to hurt you. I'm trying to help. Nox is trying to—"

"Nox?" he echoed.

I focused on my right hand and created a flame, flicking it a short distance away before allowing it to grow. I needed to see him clearly. I wanted to be sure.

The man in front of me was no older than twenty, with a small goatee doing nothing to make him seem older. He was slim but tall, a good six feet, and was wearing leather pants and a thin sweater.

His hair was tucked inside a bandanna, but I could see the edge of a tight black braid running along his hairline. His skin wasn't as dark as Nox's, but he had the same amber coloring to his eyes. "You're a shifter too?"

His eyes narrowed.

"Nox..." I trailed off, suddenly figuring out who, and what, those guys were. "Oh my god! How many of you are there?"

He blinked at me a few times before lowering the axe. "Nox? He's... are you a Dorothy?"

I shook my head. "No. Ella. I'm Dorothy's great granddaughter. Nox is a lion shifter too, he's helping me..." Realization dawned. He was here to substantiate Sayer's claims. He'd brought me with him to see for myself, one way or the other, where Sayer's loyalties truly lay. "He was sent here to find you..."

A cheer rang out from somewhere behind—a loud, echoing sound that suggested it had come from inside.

"Sounds like you're missing something," I commented, as relief surged through my chest. "I'll stay here. Go and see."

He looked at me for a moment, then dropped his weapon. It clattered to the ground and I gave him a small nod of encouragement.

He didn't say a word as he ran past me. I didn't look to see where he'd gone. Instead, I pulled up the hood of my coat, stuffed my hands back into my pockets, and sat beside the fire to wait.

CONTINUED....

ABOUT THE AUTHOR

Thank you so much for reading.
Book three in the Kingdoms of Oz series is available here
amzn.to/2G4qTyO

Join my mailing list here www.carriewhitethorne.com
Join my Facebook group here https://www.facebook.com/
groups/whitethornesworks/
Please feel free to email me with any questions, comments,
or other feedback here- enquiries @carriewhitethorne.com

Printed in Dunstable, United Kingdom